# CRUSHING THE MOB

*Mob Lust Series: Book Five*

**KRISTEN LUCIANI**

*Crushing the Mob* © 2019 by Kristen Luciani

This book is a work of fiction. Names, characters, places and incidents are the product of the author's imagination or are used fictitiously. Any resemblance to actual events, locales or persons, living or dead is purely coincidental.

Except for the original material written by the author, all songs, song titles, and lyrics mentioned in this novel are the property of the respective songwriters and copyright holders.

All rights reserved. The unauthorized reproduction or distribution of this copyrighted work is illegal. This book or any portion thereof may not be reproduced, scanned, distributed, or used in any manner whatsoever, via the Internet, electronic, or print, without the express written permission of the author, except for the use of brief quotations in a book review.

For more information, or information regarding subsidiary rights, please contact Kristen Luciani at kluciani@gmail.com

Edited by: Elaine York of Allusion Graphics

Cover Design by: Cosmic Letterz

❀ Created with Vellum

## PROLOGUE

### Katarina, Age 16

**8 YEARS AGO**

It's amazing how quickly a day can go from being damn-near perfect to something straight out of a horror movie, one that would give you nightmares for the rest of your life...

If you survived it.

"Lil! Come on, do it! You're always worrying about getting hurt. Sometimes you just need to go for it!" I yell to my sister Liliana, who is positioned on the mat at our gymnastics studio with a panicked look on her face.

She smacks her hands on her bare legs and lets out a frustrated yell. "I hate you, Kat!"

I snicker. "Yeah, yeah. Just throw it already!"

Sometimes I feel like more of a gymnastics coach than our actual coach is. And I feel like I'm the only one who can actually get Lili's body moving some days.

Today is a really important one, though. We have a big meet coming up this weekend, and Liliana is totally flaking out on her floor exercises. I get that she's recovering from an injury...one that she never would have had if our dipshit coach had been paying attention…but if Liliana doesn't get back on the horse now, he's going to gallop away forever.

"Maybe someone else should go while we wait for the Princess to decide she's ready," Tami snipes.

"Shut it, Tami. Give her a second." I let out a sigh and fold my arms across my chest, turning a glare toward Evie, our coach. She's staring at her phone, not that it would matter anyway. Tami is her spoiled brat daughter who pretty much gets away with saying and doing whatever she wants. "Let's go, Lil!" I clap my hands together loudly and stare up to the viewing window where my boyfriend Remy is watching. I shrug my shoulders and roll my eyes in his direction, and he winks back at me.

He knows I always have my twin sister's back.

I hold my breath as Lil takes a deep breath and starts running from the far corner of the mat. Her feet pound on the surface as she hurls her body into the air, her perfect form launching into a round-off, back handspring, back tuck, pausing only the slightest second before twirling into a double full before her feet hit the mat. A fabulous landing. She didn't stumble once.

She turns her wide smile to me. "Thank you," she mouths.

Coach Evie does a slow clap, and I turn away so she doesn't see me roll my eyes again. I could do her freaking job, for Pete's sake. I strut across the mat, give my sister a high five, and swivel around to cock an eyebrow at Tami. "Looks like she's got it. I'm thinking we're good for Saturday."

Evie's lips pull into a straight line. "That's for the *coach* to decide, Kat. Not you, even though you make it very clear you have no regard for my authority."

I flash a sweet smile. "Evie, that's not true at all. I just want us to win."

"You think I don't?"

I tap a finger to my cheek, knowing I'm going to get an earful from John, our head coach. I'm always the one who can't keep her mouth shut, the loud and obnoxious one who's always getting into trouble for speaking her mind...the complete opposite of my dear sweet sister. I'm much more like my father. Much more like a lion than a lamb. At least that's what my mother always says.

And that's putting it mildly.

I lean in close so only Evie can hear me. "I just think it would be nice for you to coach the rest of us when Tami isn't on the mat. Last I checked, Lili is the one who's being scouted, not her. Just saying."

Oh my God, the look on her face is so worth the crap I'm going to get for shooting off my mouth like that. The color drains from her cheeks, and her mouth drops open a little bit.

Yeah, I said it. The question is, what is she going to do about it?

"I don't know what you're talking about," she hisses, her eyes narrowed like she is plotting my death.

I shrug. "I'm pretty observant. And I think Lili needs to be first string on Saturday. Coach John will be there, too. Don't you want to impress him with a big win, since you know we need Lili to take first place?"

Evie balls her fists, and if I look really hard, I bet I can see smoke coming out of her ears. "Fine. But if she gets another mental block before then—"

I hold up a hand. "Don't worry. I've got it. I can do your job better than you can."

Oops. I didn't mean for that last part to slip out.

"You're a real bitch, you know that, Kat?"

Um, I take that back. I meant it to come out. One-hundred-and-fifty percent.

My grin widens. "Yeah. I get that a lot." I pull Lili by the hand and wave at Evie with my free one. "See you on Saturday!" I say in a sing-song voice.

If looks could kill...wow, I'd be sliced up like a pizza right about now.

Speaking of pizza...

I squeeze Lili's hand. "I'm starving. Let's get pizza! It's time to celebrate!"

She giggles. "You're going to get into so much trouble with that mouth of yours."

"Whatever. Evie is such a bitch. And she's getting fat, too. Next time she picks on you, I'm going to tell her that her ass is way too big for those Spandex pants she can't seem to stop wearing."

Lili gasps. "Kat, you can't! That's so mean!"

"What's she going to do? Take me off the team?" I wave a hand in front of my face and pull open the door to the changing room. "We're the best gymnasts she has, and she knows it. I can say whatever I want to her!"

"You really need to work on your people skills." Lili snickers, pulling on her sweats.

"I think they're just fine."

"I'm not sure the rest of the world would agree with that."

"People just don't know how to take me, that's all." I giggle. "I tell it like it is, and they don't like that."

Remy is waiting for us outside of the changing room with a smirk on his handsome face. "So did you manage to get yourself kicked off the team yet, Kat?"

I snicker. "Not today! But I'll try again next time."

Tami sails past us and glares in my direction. "You think you're such hot shit," she mutters.

I wink at her. "Damn right I do."

A snicker slips out of Lili's mouth, and she claps a hand over it.

Tami glares at her next. "Lili, I hope you can get your crap together for Saturday. You have a lot riding on this meet, don't you? I'd hate to see you choke and fall flat on your pretty face."

I clench my fists and shrug off Remy's hand from my shoulder. He sees what's coming next even if Tami misses it. "Speaking of choking..."

"Are you threatening me, Kat?" Tami puffs out her chest, her face screwed into a grimace.

"Nope. It's not a threat." I step closer, eyes narrowed, and she cowers the slightest bit.

"Guys! Enough!" Lili pushes us apart. "We're supposed to be a team, remember? Can you please just quit it already?"

My sister, the peacemaker. She can't stand to see anyone at odds. Just one more way we are complete opposites. It always shocks me to think of how different we are on the inside and how eerily alike we are on the outside.

Tami snorts and flounces down the hall. She's never been swift enough to come up with a good comeback for me. And, trust me, I give her plenty of opportunities to that she never takes.

Lili groans. "Can we please go now?"

We leave the gym and walk toward Remy's Ford F-150. He opens the doors for us, and I hop into the passenger's seat, reclining against the soft leather. I turn my adoring eyes toward my tall boyfriend as he slides into the seat next to me. "I'm thinking pizza for dinner." My voice drops. "And maybe something yummy for dessert? A little birthday treat?"

Lili makes gagging noises in the backseat. "Oh my God, can you at least wait until I'm out of the car before you start making your disgusting plans? You're making my ears bleed!"

I laugh, lacing my fingers with Remy's as he drives toward our house. I turn up the volume on the radio, singing along with Britney Spears. Life is pretty darn awesome right now.

We pull around the back of our house nestled at the end of a quiet street. It's not a huge house, but it's the perfect size for the four of us and Stoli, our chocolate lab. Dad always says you don't ever want to have the biggest house on the block. You always want to fly under the radar. Too much attention is bad. Too much attention means people are watching you. And we don't like people watching us.

I'm not sure why that is, but he says it a lot.

I think it has something to do with his job, but he doesn't talk much about that. I ask plenty, but he doesn't give me answers. Neither does Mom. Sometimes I think she's as clueless as we are about what he does.

Remy is just happy that Dad spends a lot of time away for work. Dad is pretty overprotective and he doesn't like guys who like his girls. He definitely wouldn't like what said guys *do* with his girls.

Okay, I'm just talking about myself. Lili's legs are locked at the knee.

I hop out of the passenger's seat and smile when I hear Stoli's loud barks coming from the house. Remy stays put, though. I look over at him with a questioning stare. "You're not coming in?" The corners of my lips curl upward. "I can't tempt you with something *sweet?*"

Lili rushes past me into the house, but not before she sticks a finger down her throat and makes more gagging noises.

Remy shifts in his seat. "I can't today, Kat. But I'll pick you up from school tomorrow, okay? And we'll hang out then."

My brow furrows. He's acting weird. He was fine at the gym and on the ride home. "Are you okay? You seem a little off."

He shrugs. "Got a lot of work to do, that's all."

Work. Huh. He has a job at a construction site, and as far as I know, he was done at four o'clock.

"You're going back to the site?"

"Yeah." He averts his eyes and peeks into the rearview mirror. "Listen, I've gotta go. I'll call you later. Happy birthday." He drops a quick kiss onto my lips.

"Okay." I barely have enough time to shut the door before he peels out of my driveway.

Weird. I narrow my eyes.

It's my sixteenth birthday, for Pete's sake. I know our party isn't until tomorrow night, but really? He couldn't even make time to come inside for a soda? My lips press together as I stare at the back of his truck zooming down my street. He'd better not be cheating on me. He has no clue what I'm capable of, and I'm pretty sure he doesn't want to find out.

I'm only sixteen, but I'm also Viktor Ivanov's daughter.

Dipshit won't know what hit him if he's actually stupid enough to try.

I walk into the house and slam the door shut behind me. "Hey, Mom. How about pizza tonight for dinner? Dad won't be home until late, right? I'm tired of grilled chicken and vegetables. Save the rabbit food for him. Let's party! It's our birthday!"

I wander over to the stovetop where a giant chocolate layer cake is cooling. Yum. My absolute favorite. The rich scent makes my mouth water. Pizza and chocolate. Life just doesn't get any better.

Stoli yelps and leaps at me, ready to play after being stuck in the house all day.

"Hey, boy," I croon, kneeling to rub his belly when he flips onto his back. "How about pizza tonight, huh? Doesn't that sound good? Sausage and pepperoni…mmm!"

Stoli rolls back over, his tongue hanging out of his mouth, eyes open wide. I swear he can understand English.

Mom looks up from the desk where she's tapping away at her laptop keyboard. "Okay, Kat. Make the call!"

I rub my hands together. Pizza is the very best thing on the planet. My mouth waters as I imagine biting into the cheesy goodness. Lili warns me that my addiction to bread and cheese is going to catch up to me one day, but I'll worry about it then. Right now, I'll enjoy my crazy-fast metabolism. And my loaded pizza.

I grab the phone and dial the pizza place just as the doorbell rings. Stoli goes nuts, barking and galloping across the hardwood floor to greet whoever is waiting on the other side of the door. "Lil!" I call out over my shoulder, grabbing a menu from the top drawer. I don't know why I look. I always get the exact same thing every time I place an order. "Can you get that?"

Lili pads across the hardwood floor into the foyer and pulls open the door as I put the phone to my ear.

Huh.

No dial tone.

Just dead silence.

I click it off and on again.

Nothing.

Dead.

That was my last conscious thought before all hell broke loose and my life was turned upside down and inside out.

Ironic.

*Pop! Pop! Pop!*

I twist around when I hear a loud thud by the front door, feeling as though I'm trapped in some kind of alternate reality where my limbs have turned to rubber, and I can't move. Or speak. Or scream.

All I can do is stare in horror at my dog lying limp and bloody on the floor. High-pitched shrieks pierce the air as two hulking men dressed in some kind of maintenance uniforms come barreling into the house, one grabbing my sister and slamming her against a wall, the other lunging for my mother.

The phone drops from my hand, shattering on the granite countertop, but nobody notices the sound.

Or me.

"Mom!" I yell. But I can't hear myself say the word. It sounds fuzzy and muffled, like I'm screaming into a hand. My feet are anchored to the floor, immobile. No matter how hard I try, I can't get them to move.

Tears sting my eyes as I scour the kitchen counter. The butcher block is within reach. I grit my teeth and lunge for it, grabbing a large cutting knife from the wooden slot before either of the men can get to me.

*I have to move, have to get help, have to save them!*

I drop to the floor and crawl around the island, peering at the men assaulting my mother and sister. The sounds…I know at that moment if I survive this thing, I'll never forget their horrified and panicked cries for mercy. Fabric is torn from their writhing bodies as they twist out of the grip of the men. But they're strong...so damn strong. And they have guns. I clap a hand over my mouth, bile rising in my throat.

*Help, help, help!*

*Daddy, where are you?*

My breaths come fast and furious as I feel around on the floor for my backpack. A loud yelp makes me swallow a gasp. I peek around the center island to see one of the men grab a Ming vase...my mother's prized possession...raise it up and smash it.

Right onto my mother's head.

Shattering her skull.

Lili lets out a bloodcurdling scream, her body now covered in our mother's blood, as the man wrestling with her fumbles with his belt buckle and tears off her leggings. He forces her legs open and pushes into her. Hard. More screeches as he plunders her. My hand flies to my mouth and the knife clatters to the floor as he thrusts into her, over and over and over. Tears stream down her face and my gut clenches with each push into her. The searing pain of him tearing through her innocence, her terror and anguish...my God, I feel it all.

Every little bit.

It's torture of the worst kind.

My beautiful, talented sister.

My other half.

Our perfect life.

Destroyed.

Our hopes and dreams.

Shattered.

Our loving mother.

Murdered.

I grab the handle of the knife again and try to settle my breathing. I'm the only one who can help, the only one who can stop these monsters. I crawl out from the island and rise on wobbly knees.

"Where do you think you're going with that, sweet ass?" A low voice that I don't recognize hisses next to my ear. I double over, the stench of stale alcohol stings my nostrils. Strong fingertips close tight around my wrist, digging into my flesh. "I think you're gonna wanna let go of this right now. Otherwise, you'll end up just like them."

The knife clatters to the ceramic tile at my feet, and I choke on a loud sob as the hand now closes around my throat, squeezing tight, slowly crushing my windpipe.

I gasp for air, my hands flying to my neck, desperate to pry them away. But he's too strong…this person behind me. I never saw his face, only heard his threats. That voice…low, gravelly, almost demonic…it thrums against my ear as white spots flash across my eyes.

But they only blind me for a second…not long enough for me to miss the streaks of red that stain my blurred vision.

So much blood.

So much devastation.

So much loss.

My perfect life.

Over.

## *Chapter One*

## KATARINA

I pucker my perfectly lined, deep red lips one last time before sliding a pair of Chanel sunglasses onto my nose. It's cloudy outside. There's not one sliver of sunshine peeking through the overcast sky, but they preserve my anonymity.

Temporarily, until I decide it's time for my identity to be known.

Nobody ever sees it coming.

Fucking idiots.

They think they can get away with not paying their debts. They think they can get away with the lying, cheating, and stealing.

They never remember that someone always comes to collect.

And it never ends well for the ones who violate the rules.

I step out of my gleaming black Maserati...well, it's not mine, but one of our fleet. It has no trace whatsoever to me or my father with its Pennsylvania plates. It's registered to one of our shell companies, and ownership of said company is in the sole paws of Stoli, my beloved and deceased chocolate lab.

I smooth down the hair of my blonde wig. The waves cascade down my back, over the ivory trench coat that covers my tight black dress. I adjust the sunglasses with one manicured hand and my Jimmy Choo stilettos click and clack along the pavement outside of the nondescript building down in the Diamond District in lower Manhattan.

It's after hours, so the streets in the surrounding area are pretty much deserted. The city clears out once the workday ends, and this area is no exception.

Except if you have a private appointment, which I do. A smile plays at my lips when I ring the bell.

He's expecting me.

But I can guarantee he's not anticipating what's about to enter his domain.

A large security guard comes to the door and unlatches it to allow me entry.

Stupid motherfucker.

I could be anyone.

Literally.

I step inside, my heels sinking into the carpet. My red lips curl upward as I regard the beefy security guard. Ian Raines should have kept two guards on duty tonight, just for good measure.

He is such a cheap bastard.

Ironic that it's gonna cost him a hell of a lot more than the regular time and a half for his security detail.

The guard doesn't speak to me. He just stands there, trying to look menacing. I flash a smile in his direction, and he doesn't even blink in response.

He'll be sorry he wasn't nicer to me.

I step into the dimly lit space, eyeing the jewelry casings lining the walls. Raines doesn't keep much on display. He has most of the prized items safely locked up in a back viewing room.

A room reserved for his best customers.

He thinks he's going to make a killing back there.

He has no idea that it will be the other way around.

Raines appears a few moments later, a sly smile on his face when he sees me. "Ms. Blake. Such a pleasure to see you."

I offer him my hand, and he brushes his lips against it. I fight the urge to break his wrist and pummel him into the middle of next week.

Rage issues. They never really subsided over the past eight years. I think they've gotten worse, actually.

"Hello, Mr. Raines. Thank you for agreeing to open for me on such short notice. I'm boarding a flight back to Europe tonight, and I couldn't leave New York without seeing your new collection." I unbelt my trench and slowly slide it off of my shoulders, tossing it on a chair. I walk toward him, rubbing myself against him as I lean to look at a piece in one of the cases below.

His breath is hot against my ear. "Don't waste your time looking at those. I have many, many others that are much more worthy of a beautiful woman like you." He nods his head toward the viewing room, which my surveillance already told me was in the far-left corner of the storefront. "Let me show you." He turns toward the security guard. "Nick, you can go. I'll take it from here." He crosses the floor and locks the door behind Nick, his only source of security and protection.

Cheap bastard. He's really going to wish he hadn't done that.

I follow him into the viewing room. He bolts the door behind us and adjusts a set of cameras that cover multiple views of the storefront and the outside. He grins at me. "This is just a safety precaution. With the push of a button, I can have the cops here in seconds."

Raines doesn't need to worry about what is happening outside of his place.

Because I work alone.

In my experiences, men just fuck everything up anyway.

I'm better off by myself, collecting what people owe us and destroying the ones who take from us.

I always get the job done.

It's why my father trusts me as his number one.

What Raines should have been more focused on was the mysterious young woman who showed up at his door, instead of any crew she might be working with.

But that's what happens when you get sloppy, and when you're too money-hungry to think about the consequences of your actions.

"So the cameras serve as your security guard, hmm?" I ask, fluffing out my fake blonde hair with a black leather-gloved hand. "You're not scared of little old me? You're willing to put your trust in a complete stranger?" I keep my tone light and flirtatious. There's no hint of an accent, either. Another little trick I've perfected.

The corners of Raines's lips lift upward into a sinister smile. He reaches under the desk and places a gun on the table next to him. "Of course, Miss Blake. My complete trust is right here next to me."

I smile, running a finger over the semiautomatic pistol. Too bad he forgot to remove the safety. "Oohh, the scent of death and the sparkle of diamonds," I say in a breathy voice. "I love it."

"You can't be too careful in this business." Raines folds his arms across his chest. "Now what can I show you? I believe you said you wanted to wrap this up quickly to make your flight."

I never said anything like that. He's squirming. I think it might be time...

"Well..." I pretend to think for a second. "I'd love to see something that really pops, you know? Like maybe the shipment of cocaine your organization intercepted and stole from my father before it hit Miami?" I look around. "Did you save any of that? Or have you sold it already and buried the cash?"

The color all but drains from his face, and he grabs the gun, pointing it at me.

"Tsk-tsk, Raines," I say, pulling off my glasses and dropping them onto the table. "And after he gave you a massive loan to fund your new jewelry collection. You couldn't get that money from anyone else because you're a lying, manipulative scumbag who can't be trusted. My father saved your ass, and how do you thank him? By fucking him over. You used his money to fund your little plan. I bet you thought it was poetic justice, right?" I eye the gun he's pointing toward me and smirk.

"I took back what was rightfully mine. Your father crushed my business. He forced me out of the game. Well, fuck him. What I stole is nothing compared to what he's about to lose. He's got a lot of enemies, Ms. Ivanov. And rest assured, when they hear about this little stunt of yours, they will not be happy." He walks out from behind the desk, still holding the gun tight in his hand. He slides his free one down my torso and over my hips. I grit my teeth and let the asshole manhandle me for a second. I want him to feel comfortable that I have nothing to hide.

And regretful that he should've pulled the trigger when he had the chance.

Sucker.

I slip away from him in a blink, hooking an arm around his neck to cut off circulation. I bring my other hand down hard over the one he's clutching the gun in, slicing at it with all the strength I can muster. The gun clatters to the floor.

Shock and awe.

It's my trademark.

They never see me coming.

Raines gasps for air, writhing against me as I pull harder. "Never bite the hand that feeds you, Raines. Because if you do, it'll always come back and bite you back. *Hard*."

I tighten my arms around his neck, yank, and pull, waiting for the satisfying crack before I drop Raines face-down on the floor.

I check the security footage and confirm that the immediate area is still desolate before opening the door a crack. I keep one eye on the store while I fumble around with his security system to delete the feeds for the past thirty minutes and empty the trash on his computer so that there is no trace of me or my car in this vicinity.

Miss Blake?

Erased from existence.

I finish hacking his system, shut it down, and smooth the front of my dress before stepping over Raines and leaving the viewing room. I grab my trench and slide it on before unlocking the front door and strutting out of the store.

Once I'm safely in my borrowed car, I let out a deep breath, tears stinging my eyes. I let it happen. I watched them die. I saw my life crumble right in the middle of our beautiful home, and I couldn't stop it.

That knowledge has haunted me every day since my sixteenth birthday.

Raines's last words ring out in my tortured mind.

*What I stole is nothing compared to what he's about to lose.*

No loss compares to the one we suffered eight years ago. No amount of money can bring my mother and sister back.

And no matter how many of our debts I collect, no matter how many enemies I destroy, I know none of it will make us whole again.

## Chapter Two

# ROCCO

"Hick-fucking-ville." I hop out of my black Chevy Commander and look around at the green, grassy fields surrounding us. "I hope you brought your cowboy boots and spurs."

Nico Salesi, the head of the Salesi crime family and one of my best friends, snickers, following me over to the fence along the property. I climb on the bottom rung and lean over, breathing in the fresh air. I almost choke, I inhale so deeply.

"Easy, killer. This air is pure, not like the shit you've been inhaling back home for most of your life."

The wind whips through my hair, and I pull my baseball cap from the back pocket of my jeans, sticking it on my head. I turn around to face Nico and fold my hands across my chest. "So why the hell are we here in Bumblefuck, New Jersey? I mean, I know you like the track, but I didn't think you wanted to buy and race your own ponies."

"I don't."

"Okay." I nod and look at the large white house in the distance. Four stories high, red shutters, picket fence. "Are you so sick of us that you're planning to move Shaye up here?" I chuckle. "Or are you so sick of *me* that you decided to ship me off to God's country to live off the land?"

"You're getting warmer."

I roll my eyes. Nico doesn't give a fucking inch when he doesn't want to. But I'd really like to know why I'm about to be neck-deep in horse shit. Literally.

As if I don't have enough other crap to deal with. Like my survival.

"Let's go inside."

"Why? Do you think the animals are gonna hear about whatever your plans are and run straight to the feds?"

"No, dipshit. I need to take a leak."

"Aha, running water. Nice, so it's at least somewhat civilized up here."

"I told you you'd love it."

"Yeah, but you didn't tell me I'd be taking up residence."

Nico nods his head toward the massive farmhouse. "Come on. Take a load off, partner."

"Christ, you even sound like a cowboy now."

We walk along the cobblestone pathway toward the house, and Nico pulls out a key, shoving it into the lock and twisting the knob. The bright red door creaks open, and a musty smell wafts over us. I wrinkle my nose. "Smells like my grandma's old house."

"Your grandma's old house smelled like escarole and sauce, dude."

"Yeah, when she was *cooking*. I'm talking about the rest of the time."

Nico shakes his head and starts opening doors. I guess he's looking for the bathroom. He opens a few down a hallway and disappears for a minute.

I peer into the rooms on the first floor. All of the furniture is covered in plastic...Jesus, I really feel like I'm in the Twilight Zone now. Grandma always had her shit covered in plastic. I remember hating to sit down in the living room in the summer time. My grandparents never used the air conditioner. When my Pop was sick, she'd keep it off so he wouldn't get a chill. Then after he died, she just never bothered to turn it on again. I guess she got used to the sweltering heat. But damn, I remember how my legs would stick to the plastic and sear the skin any time I'd visit in the hot summer months.

I tried not to visit too often between the spring and fall for that reason.

Now she lives down in Florida, without the plastic, and I visit all year round because she turns on the air conditioner in the ninety-plus-degree temps.

Nico curses loudly and a loud banging sound vibrates the walls of the house. "Nico, what the hell did you do in there? It sounds like the pipes are revolting!"

He pops his head out of the bathroom. "Realtor never turned on the water."

"Gross, man. I'll hold it until we get back on the road." I brush past him and walk into the kitchen. Sunlight streams into a solarium in the back of the house and the light bounces off of the shiny surfaces of the room. It's quiet. Peaceful. And nothing at all like I'm used to.

Why the hell am I here again?

Still waiting for a fucking answer.

"Am I being whacked?" I turn toward Nico. "Is that why you brought me to the place where elephants go to die? Am I joining them?"

Nico lets out a frustrated sigh. "No, dick. If I wanted you dead, you'd already be in the ground."

I pull out a chair at the kitchen table and drum my fingertips on the wood grain. "Okay, I'm out of guesses, bro."

"So then just be patient and stop with the fucking Spanish Inquisition!"

I throw my hands in the air. "Fine! I'll just sit here and wait for you to decide what you want to tell me and when."

Nico pulls his cell phone from his pocket, catching it on the first ring. "Yeah." Pause. "We're both here. Waiting for you. Okay."

*Click.*

A minute passes, and I keep drumming.

Nico cocks an eyebrow at me. "That phone call didn't make you any bit curious?"

I slam a hand on the table. "Of course it did! But I know if I ask the question, you'll give me some one-word bullshit answer. Why bother? I'd rather just save my breath."

"I'm glad you're learning some self-control." Nico pulls out a chair and sits across from me. "That was Viktor on the phone, by the way."

My ears perk up. Viktor Ivanov, as in head of one of the most powerful bosses of the Russian mafia. As in badass drug lord who lives on what appears to be an exclusively black cigarette and vodka-based diet.

He's dangerous. And manipulative. And vicious.

Dark hair, ice-blue eyes that can pierce as deep as the knives he's been rumored to wield like a butcher slicing up livestock.

Livestock. Funny, you know, because of where we are right now.

Viktor and Nico have worked together for the past few years. I don't know much about him personally, only what I've heard. And none of it is good if you're on his shit list.

He's got a lot of enemies, nasty ass people who brutalize for shits and giggles. I'm talking, stick a fork in your fucking eye and yank it out kind of brutal. And for people who associate with Viktor? It's like guilt by association.

And here I am, about to take a meeting with him.

But that's nothing compared to what I've already done on his behalf.

Because of that, his enemies have become my enemies.

Fucking fabulous.

Five years ago, I was just trying to make some fast cash. I had no idea I'd have a target on my back because of it. I've done some pretty underhanded things back in the day, things other people might have gotten their dicks chopped off for. But I always landed on my feet.

I was an idiot for thinking this time would be different.

I always think I can escape. Maybe that's because I've been lucky.

But luck is pretty damn fleeting.

And these enemies...they will always find what they're looking for. You can't hide, can't protect yourself. Pretty much the only thing you can do is pray.

But even God can't stop the inevitable.

I've seen it play out more times than I can count.

The first time they came, we conquered.

The next time?

I don't really know if Lady Luck is gonna stick around for that.

"Who's he bringing?" I ask the question, trying to keep my voice disinterested in the answer even though I'm silently willing him to say the name I want to hear.

A sly smile lifts his lips. "Sorry. She's not coming. He'll be alone."

Nico, that asshole. He's too damn perceptive for his own good.

I let out a snort, pretending not to care that Katarina, Viktor's daughter and chief assassin, won't be joining us for this meeting. The truth is, I really want to see her. Bitch is cold as ice but white hot at the same time. I haven't been able to think of much else since she wiggled her tight ass into Jersey and everyone knows it. I've been called out plenty of times by the guys for staring a little too long, making excuses to tag her in for a quick poker game or a necessary ass kicking. But she's got poison running through her veins. Poison and vodka. I think she likes knowing every man within a ten-mile radius wants to get her on her back. But she keeps her distance, especially from me. And it only makes me want her more. "I wasn't asking about

Kat. I was just curious to see if anyone else was in on the reason for this secret meeting."

"Sure you were." Nico winks at me and scrolls through his phone.

I roll my eyes. "That's all I get? Viktor is coming?"

He shrugs. "Hey, you wanted information."

What I'd really like to know, and Nico will only tell me once he's good and ready, is how the hell I'm gonna survive the planned hit on my life, and how this goddamn horse farm is involved.

A car door slams out front, and a minute later, Viktor strides into the kitchen. He's wearing all black.

Always all black.

Ominous. Commanding.

Death.

Every time I look at him, I imagine it's what the devil would look like if he walked the Earth. No shit, he's that bad.

Nico nods at him but doesn't get out of his seat.

I do, though. I get up and take a few steps backward to lean against the counter. For some reason, I need distance. I feel like maybe it gives me back a tiny bit of control.

Not that it matters.

These guys have a plan. It's pretty obvious. And the plan is gonna put my head on the chopping block.

Again.

Fuck my life.

But this is what I signed up for years ago when Nico's grandfather saved my ass.

Sometimes I think it would have been easier if he'd have just had me capped. Then I wouldn't have to keep looking over my shoulder, wondering when, where, how...

Because I sure as hell already know the *who*.

It's the same *who* that wants Viktor.

Viktor looks at me, his blue eyes narrowed. "You might want to take a seat."

"Thanks, I'm good here." I try to keep my voice strong. Confident.

I'm bullshitting myself and everyone else in the room.

Viktor pulls out a chair and lowers himself into it. Everything the man does is calculated and deliberate. He's not rash and impulsive like his daughter, who will leap at the chance to put some poor sucker in a deadly chokehold because of the way he's talking to her friend.

Yeah, she's done that to me.

My lips stretch into a thin line.

Shit, I'm doing it again. I can't think about Katarina right now, not that she's ever far from my mind. I wonder at least a hundred times a day when she's gonna swoop in wearing obscenely tight jeans and a low-cut shirt to plug some dickhead who was stupid enough to be in the wrong place at the wrong time. I'm not complaining. Watching someone get the shit kicked out of him by a girl who looks like a Victoria's Secret model is hot as fuck.

And since Nico and Viktor have formed this Italian-Russian mob boss partnership thing, she's been showing up on the scene more and more.

Looking hotter and hotter.

I grasp the countertop that I'm leaning against and swallow hard.

My fucking life is hanging in the balance right now, and all I can focus on is *her*.

It's not like I can't occupy myself with others. There are always others. I work at Nico's nightclub, Culaccino, and believe me, there's plenty of pussy on display in that sex den. But it's too easy. There's no challenge in getting laid there. Yeah, I can get off, but it's boring.

I didn't always feel that way, though. Not until Katarina Ivanov torpedoed her way into my life. She ruined it for every other female out there for me who was ready to drop her panties and spread her legs.

I have to stop these X-rated images from flying through my mind. If Viktor could see what's wallpapering my brain right now, I'm sure he'd happily take one of the knives in the butcher block to my left and stab me in the eye—and maybe even the dick, for good measure—with it.

"Thanks for coming, Viktor." Nico places his phone on the table and looks over at me. "Are you joining us?"

"No offense, but I feel like I need to be standing to hear what comes next."

A smirk plays at Viktor's lips. "What's the plan?"

Nico stares at me for a few seconds before speaking. My heart hammers. He's got a plan. That's a good thing. It doesn't guarantee I'll survive, but hearing that there actually is a 'plan?'

Promising.

Nico turns back to Viktor. "Everything is set up for the horse farm. Groundskeepers, on-staff veterinarians, trainers, insurance, stable hands...they all have business accounts set up where we'll wire their salaries, cushioned with our cut. We'll purchase horses under the new shell company and start paying salaries and insurance premiums to the crew to justify the care and maintenance of the animals and farm." He points a finger to me without stopping for a breath. "Rocco will oversee the operation from here."

"Who, whoa, whoa." I hold up my hands. "I thought this was a meeting to discuss how the fuck we're gonna handle the Cinque family and keep them from slicing me into carpaccio. I already have a job, remember? I was only kidding about you sending me out here to die."

"I'm sending you here to keep that from happening. That's what this meeting is about," Nico replies in a serious voice.

"Wait, so I'm just supposed to become a cowboy now? Leave the city to herd fucking cattle? What the hell is next? Are you gonna throw some flannel shirts and a Stetson at me, too? How exactly is this supposed to preserve my life?"

"Nobody said anything about cows, although..." Nico rubs the scruff on his chin. "That's not a bad way to expand the business once things get going. Definitely keeps us off the radar if we become ranchers..."

"Oh, come the fuck on!" I slam my hands on the counter. "Is all this really necessary?"

Nico rises from his chair, the legs scraping against the floor. "I don't know, Rocco. Do you like the idea of your mouth being pulled through your asshole? Is that a nice visual? Because I can guarantee that would be a picnic compared to what the Cinques will do once they find you."

"They haven't gotten to me yet," I grumble, pulling off my baseball cap and shoving it on backwards. I do that a lot when I'm stressed. As if the position of the goddamn cap can change my suck-ass predicament.

"They're coming," Viktor says in a low voice.

"Look, I got what you needed when I was out in California. Now you know where their operations are. You know who's running shit out there." I pause for a second, struggling to keep my voice calm, but damn, it's hard. "I did what Grandpa Vito asked me to do. I went to the Cinques, pretending that you guys kicked me out of Jersey, that I was pissed off, and wanted revenge. They bought it, and I got in deep enough to find out who put the hit on your family, Vik. Now they're after both of us. So why are we sitting around holding our dicks waiting for them to show up on our doorstep? Why don't we just take them the fuck out already?"

Nico lets out a deep sigh and rakes a hand through his hair. But he says nothing.

That means he doesn't want to show his hand.

Well, screw that. My ass is on the line. I did what I had to do for the family. But is the family gonna do anything for me? That's the big question.

"Nico," I say, struggling to keep my voice even. "I don't want to talk about horses. I want to know why I'm here."

Viktor turns his penetrating gaze to me. "You're here because you're going to do a job for us."

"No disrespect, Vik, but I think I've done plenty."

Nico grits his teeth and glares at me. "Sit the fuck down, Rocco."

I pull out a chair and flop into it. "Happy?"

"Here's the deal." Nico taps on the tabletop with his fingertips. "Our location isn't hidden. Everyone in the organization knows we own Jersey and everything south of it. We don't operate outside of those locations. It makes us easy to find. But this place, this farm, is outside of our regular territory."

"Thanks for the geography lesson," I quip.

Nobody cracks a smile.

Shocker.

Ironic that the primary target is the one trying to lighten this situation.

"The point is, there is no affiliation between the farm to our other businesses. This is separate. Buried. Off the radar." He pauses. "Undetectable."

"Who knows about it?"

"The three of us." Nico and Viktor exchange glances.

"That's all?" I furrow my brow.

"Yep. For now."

"And I'm going to be stuck up here?"

"Think of it as a refuge from fucking mutilation of the worst imaginable kind." Nico rolls his eyes. "Do you get what I'm doing here? I'm saving your ass from the Cinques."

"For how long? I mean, this is like witness protection shit except it isn't orchestrated by the government, yeah?"

Another secret, wordless look is exchanged.

"You guys wanna let me in on the timeline? Am I turning hick or what?"

"You're going to have to stay up here for a while," Nico says, avoiding my eyes.

"How are you gonna explain my disappearance to everyone? Where the fuck am I supposed to be? What am I telling my family? This is my fucking *life*, Nico!"

Nico shoots up from his chair and leans in real close. Close enough that I can see the fire in his eyes. He's pissed, but fuck that. So am I. I'm in this shit storm because of him, his father, and his grandfather. And he's basically telling me my life as I know it is over.

What I did wasn't even that bad. I started taking sports bets without permission. Big goddamn deal. Max Oriani made it into a bigger thing than it needed to be. He's the one who ratted me out in the first place. Jealous asshole. He knew I was making more than he ever could, so he ran to Nico's Grandpa Vito, the big boss, and boom. I'm outta business.

But instead of getting beaten to death with a baseball bat, I got a punishment assignment that assured me death by baseball bat would be much more enjoyable.

I stand by what I did with the gambling. I had a good reason, not that anyone bothered to ask. They all just assumed I did it because I don't give a damn about anyone but myself and that I'm a selfish asshole.

What they didn't know was that I did it to help my grandmother pay off my Pop's medical bills when he was sick. I knew my dad was strapped, so when I overheard them talking one night, the idea came to me. I knew I'd clear enough to help, and I also knew Grandma would never ask me. So I took it upon myself and decimated Max's little betting business.

To this day, Max doesn't know the truth, and that's fine. It's none of his business. None of anyone's business. I never told Nico's dad or grandfather why I did it. It wasn't important. I did what I had to do for my family. The bills were paid, and my grandma was able to mourn my Pop without having to worry about his debts.

But what the Salesis made me do as punishment was way worse than taking those bets ever was. I went into the lion's den, surrounded by hellfire and brimstone, and I didn't think I'd make it out alive.

And now this.

"You're lucky you still have a life, Rocco! So while you're pissing and moaning about how shitty your existence will be while you hide out here, think about the fact that you'll still be fucking breathing!"

"Forget it, Nico. This plan can't work. Not with him. He's too reckless and too many risks have already been taken," Viktor says in a low, menacing voice. He stands up and walks toward me. His blue eyes are so light and so clear, they look soul-less. I can't tear my own eyes away. His stare pins me to the spot and my throat constricts, my body fully unprepared for any assault he might launch. I'm trapped by his cold, hardened gaze with no hope of breaking away.

He gets right in my face, searching me for something...I'm not sure what and he doesn't bother to give me a clue, either. He's a man of few words. He doesn't need to use many. His expressions pretty much tell you everything you need to know.

And from the looks of it, I'm fucked.

Somehow or other.

Nico lets out a frustrated sigh. "Once he understands the situation, he'll—"

Viktor pulls away from me, his gaze unwavering, lips stretched into a tight line. His eyes never leave my face as he speaks the words in his signature harsh, Russian-accented tone.

"No. He is not the one."

Then he turns and walks out of the house, slamming the door behind him.

My hand flies to my throat. I've never been strangled by a look before, and it doesn't feel fabulous.

Not the one for *what?*

## Chapter Three
# KATARINA

I flex my fingers to get the blood circulating again before balling my fists and holding them up close to my face. Perspiration drizzles down the sides of my head, and I use an arm to push back my hair.

"You need a break?" Alexi, my father's number two, grins at me and nods to a chair in the deserted gym. "Go on, sit down. Relax."

"Fuck you, Alexi." I narrow my eyes and straighten to my full height, which is damn close to his. "I'm ready."

He holds up his wrapped hands, bouncing back and forth in a boxer-ready stance. His eyes narrow as he edges closer to me. I know he hates to go full force on me, but it's required. Not like he has much of a shot since I pretty much kick his ass every time we spar.

And he really doesn't have a choice, anyway. He's been my punching bag for as long as I can remember.

Besides, if Viktor Ivanov gives you an order, you follow it. Period. No room for negotiations.

I whip out my fist, and it collides with his midsection. He swipes at me with a fist, but I back away just in time. He may be strong, but I'm fast. And speed is what counts right now. Seizing the opportunity to launch a strike at just the right time is what separates the winners from the losers.

And the killers and their victims.

I'd seen it firsthand.

I wasn't able to do anything about it then. I didn't have the skills.

Or the drive.

Or the rage.

Now I have all three, and I never plan on missing that opportunity ever again.

While his hand is away from his face, I twist to the side and shoot out my foot, hitting him square in the jaw.

I bet he wishes he'd put on his head gear right about now.

But I'm not finished with him yet. Another kick to the neck and then one power shot to the groin before he comes crashing to his knees.

I drop down in front of him, my chest heaving. I tear off my hand wraps and throw them at him with a smirk. "Looks like you're the one who needs the rest now, huh?" I pant.

Alexi rolls over and groans. "You know, I didn't sign up for this shit, Katarina. When your father assigned me gym duty, I thought I was just gonna get to watch you work out in those tight pants."

I giggle and towel off my face. "Well, I'm still working out and wearing these tight pants."

Alexi struggles to his feet. "Yeah, but now I'm sterile because of all the hits I've taken to the balls from you. You have a lot of hate down deep, babe."

I square my shoulders. That's the understatement of the century. "I keep telling you to wear the damn cup I bought you."

He snickers. "It doesn't fit. I told you I need the extra-large one."

I nearly choke on the water I'm gulping. It sprays out of my mouth, dribbling down my chin. A fit of laughter bubbles in my chest, and pretty soon I'm gasping for air. "Enough fun stuff. I need a shower."

"If my balls weren't so purple from the bruises, they'd be blue."

This whole conversation is bordering on the incestual, if you ask me. I mean, he's my best friend, and we practically grew up together.

But...he's still a guy. And I do look damn good in these Lululemons.

Alexi has always had a soft spot for me. His father used to work for my dad years ago but died in some kind of an accident. I don't know the details, and Alexi never spoke of them...or his dad. His mother went back to Russia, and my father took Alexi under his wing.

I always thought that was odd. I can't imagine my own mother leaving me and Lili with a stranger like that if she'd had the choice, but this life makes you do things you wouldn't under normal circumstances.

Normal circumstances. I'd like to know what those are...

I toss the hand towel at him. "You're lucky I like you. Otherwise, I'd have my father cut off your dick."

"I'm not in the business of butchering anymore."

I spin around, my father's deep voice echoing in the empty space. "Papa! I didn't know you'd be dropping by."

"Leave us." Papa eyes Alexi, who limps off to the locker room without hesitation. Papa may not be in the butchering department *anymore*, but he still knows how to wield a cleaver. And nobody is ever completely safe from his wrath, including Alexi.

I flop into a chair and let out a deep breath. I guess the shower will have to wait. "What's up?"

Papa folds his arms and leans against a column. In his Armani ensemble. With his black hair and ice blue eyes he looks more like an elusive billionaire than a mob boss. "Where were you last night?"

I square my shoulders in anticipation of the storm that's coming. "I went into the city."

His eyes narrow. "Where in the city?"

I spring up from my chair. In situations like these, it's best to go toe to toe with Viktor Ivanov. It shows strength. Sometimes stupidity, but mostly strength. And since I went behind his back and against his wishes with Raines, it's best that I stand tall before he shoots me down. "I went to see an old friend."

"Really," Papa hisses, inching closer. "What would you say if I told you it wasn't just your old friend who spent some quality time with you? What if I told you that someone else was there, too? Someone who took pictures of you?"

"Not possible." I wave my hand in the air. "Nobody would know it was me. I wore a wig and used a car that can't be traced—"

I try to play it off, but I can't believe this is happening. I've never been sloppy before. How could anyone have known it was me with Raines? Mere surveillance wouldn't have given away my identity!

And who the fuck are we even talking about?

I have so many faceless enemies…sometimes it's a little hard to walk around in the light of day.

You just never know…

"Katarina," he growls. "I told you to stay away from Raines. I told you to let it go!"

"I couldn't, okay?" Angry tears spring to my eyes. I clench my fists. "He took from us! They all did! He needed to pay!"

Papa grabs my shoulders and gives me a shake. "That's not how this works. I give the orders, do you understand? You don't decide who pays and who doesn't. It's not up to you!" he roars.

My lips stretch into a tight line, teeth clenched. "He's a scumbag who had a debt to pay."

"That's right. But not only to us. The people who tracked you want their money. Raines owed them."

"He owed everyone! What the hell do they want from us?"

Eyebrows knitted, Papa frowns at me. "Payment."

"So we're supposed to settle up for Raines?" I let out a snort. "Are they insane? We're not paying anyone off! We got screwed by him, too!"

"Killing him doesn't erase the debt. That's the message they sent."

"And if we don't pay?" I fold my arms across my chest.

"Don't you understand? We *will* pay!" Papa's voice chills my insides.

Fuck.

"They aren't looking for money. Not anymore. When you killed Raines, when you disobeyed my orders, *you* became the payment!" Papa shouts.

I choke on the water I'm guzzling. "Me?" I sputter.

He nods. "Yes. You. This is exactly why I wanted you to stay away from him. But you never listen! How am I supposed to trust you if you can't follow simple instructions?"

"Papa, he tried to crush us!"

"And now because of you, his enemies have become our enemies. And *they* want to crush us." He runs a hand through his dark hair and walks over to the window. "Katarina, I told you in the beginning you had to be very careful. You needed to listen to me. To trust me!"

"Papa, I do trust you. But if we let him take from us, how does that make us look?"

"That's not up to you. I am the one who determines how we handle pieces of shit like Raines. You cannot see beyond the tip of your nose!"

"I'm looking out for us!"

"No!" he yells. "You're looking for vengeance! Anywhere you can get it!"

"Why aren't you?" I whisper. Why is it only when I've gotten my father so riled up over some stupid stunt that he brings up what happened? Why can't we grieve like a normal fucking family? Why can't we talk about what happened and how it's turned us into cold and detached business associates instead of a father and daughter suffering the biggest loss they can imagine?

He closes his eyes for a second and takes a deep breath. "Katarina, there is no vengeance to be had. What happened was not because of my business. The police said it was a random break-in by some thugs who were looking for quick cash so they could buy drugs. We've gone over this again and again. What are you looking for? When will you accept it?"

Tears spill over, streaming down my face. I cover my face with my hand, trying to hide my anguish. I know damn well what I was told.

I just don't believe it to be true. I can't accept it. Any time some underworld slug tries to fuck us over, I feel the urge to destroy. Somewhere out there, the fuckers who took my mother and sister are lurking. And I will find them.

I know they're still out there.

I also know they won't stop until they put an end to the rest of the Ivanovs.

The only thing I don't know is why, and that's what I've struggled with over the past eight years.

Why did they come after us?

Why did they kill Mom and Lili?

Why did they spare me?

Why, why, why?

"Stop that crying now!" Papa grunts. "There is no room for weakness in this life. That's the first thing I taught you. You never show weakness, do you understand? And when you act out of vengeance, it makes you vulnerable."

I nod, swiping the tears from my cheeks.

Papa stares out at the city street, at the buildings in our view, pondering something. He does this a lot. Sometimes I think it's because he needs to take a break from looking at me. He needs some kind of a distraction since I'm a carbon-copy of everything he lost. My mother, sister, and I could have been triplets.

Eight years gone, but God, it feels like just yesterday Lili and

I were bouncing into our house on our sixteenth birthday, excited for a future that we'd never get to experience.

At least, together.

Sometimes I have a hard time looking at myself, too.

"You need to leave."

"What do you mean, leave?" My head snaps up, eyes wide. "I'm not going anywhere!"

His eyes dart toward me. "If I say you leave, you leave."

"Where the hell am I supposed to go? I have a life here!"

"If you want a life at all, you need to be smarter about how you handle simple instructions."

"Great." I walk over to the heavy bag and pound on it. It hurts without my hand wraps, but a little pain is good for the soul. I jab it a few more times for good measure and wince as my hand snaps against the leather. "So now what? You just ship me off somewhere. To Siberia?" I gasp. "No, please tell me I'm not going there."

Papa glares at me. "I want you to lay low until I can make arrangements, yes? If you need to go anywhere, you take Alexi. I don't want you to be alone."

"Is this really necessary? It's not like I've ever gone into hiding before, and I think we both know I've done way worse than this. You keep letting these scumbags get away with taking more and more from us. I don't understand why you won't talk to me about it. I know you have reasons, but dammit, I want to know what they are! Besides, if they come after me, I'm more than capable of taking care of myself. You *did* see Alexi when you came in, didn't you? And I went easy on him today."

"You went after the wrong person for the wrong reasons. Again! And my reasons shouldn't matter to you. I have a reason for every single action I take...for every directive I give! The money is easy to overlook when you think about the consequences. Raines stole from us, but worse than that, he had vicious enemies. Now those enemies are *our* enemies." He steps closer to me. "And the loss isn't even a consideration. No amount of money can compare to keeping you safe." His voice, while gruff, is also thick with emotion. Emotion that makes my gut clench. Emotion that I haven't heard in a very long time. In fact, it's been so long, it may just be a memory I concocted and revisit whenever I want to feel like I actually have a parent who cares about me as more than just a hired gun.

Yeah, I've got more kills than the rest of his guys combined, but I'm still his daughter. Sometimes, I like to know that he remembers that, too.

I swallow hard. I messed up. And now I have to deal with the fallout.

But it doesn't stop me from pressing on.

Because I'm just a glutton for punishment.

I wipe the sweat drizzling down the side of my face with my arm. "If you let me stay, I can bait them."

"Are you crazy? Do you realize how dangerous that is?"

"Let them try to come after me! I've lost so much, I don't even care anymore!" I stomp in a circle around my father, my sneakers pounding on the cold concrete floor. "I'll take them all down!"

Papa scrubs a hand down the front of his face. I know he's trying to control his own rage right now...maybe because Alexi is close by, maybe because he realizes it won't do him any good to lash out at me. "Katarina, this anger is dangerous! It grows deeper with each passing year, and it will be the cause your demise if you don't get control of it! I do everything in my power to keep you safe and protected. If you want to stay alive, you will listen to me!"

A large lump forms in my throat. I try to swallow past it, but I can't. It's too big, too suffocating. I can't breathe, and the sob caught in my chest slowly chokes me.

The guilt is excruciating. I wear it like a noose around my goddamn neck.

I know exactly why I went against his will, why I can't let go of the possibility that one of our enemies was responsible for killing my family.

I vowed to myself years ago that I'd take them all out, one by one.

I don't believe it was a random break-in. I never did.

Someone is responsible, and that elusive *someone* is going to pay.

I knew exactly what I was doing when I went to see Raines.

It happens every year on the same day when I allow the rage to consume me. It blinds me and mutes all sensibilities.

I ignore my role.

I ignore my allegiance to my father.

I ignore my responsibilities.

For one single day.

Yesterday.

Our birthday.

*My* birthday.

He wants to send me away to protect me.

How ironic that all I want is to be found by the people I've hunted for the past eight years.

They will find me. I'll make sure of that.

And I'll also make sure they will suffer the same fate that Mom and Lili did.

## Chapter Four

## ROCCO

"Since when do you care about God's furry creatures?" My younger sister Lindy exclaims when I pull my car into an animal shelter a few towns away from our house. "Who are you and where's my brother?"

It's been twenty-four hours and radio silence from Nico. I haven't left the house since I got back from our road trip to the farm, but today, I'm going stir-crazy. I need to get the hell outside. And I'm packing, just in case. I know I shouldn't have brought Lindy. It was a stupid call to put her in the line of fire, but she can be a pushy pain in the ass sometimes and she insisted on coming with me. It's not like I can tell her some wacked-out enemy family on the other side of the country is hunting me for being a traitor and a rat. It just means there won't be a Starbucks stop in our future. She has no idea what I do and what my dad used to do, and that's for the best. "Listen, smartass, it wasn't me who never wanted a dog. It was Mom who said we'd never take care of a dog."

"You aren't exactly the type to use a Pooper Scooper," Lindy quips. "You're going to be okay walking a dog early in the morning and late at night? And carrying its crap in a little plastic baggie *after* you've cleaned it up?"

I shrug. "Who says anything about walking a dog? I've got a fenced-in yard." Not that I'll be staying there much longer...I just hope it'll be by my choice and not someone else's.

But Lindy doesn't know that. Nobody does. Hell, I still haven't gotten Nico to commit to specifics yet.

I figure having a dog can't hurt while I wait to get my next directive from Nico, especially a badass one that nobody wants. He'll be nice and pissed off. Ready to attack any assholes who come calling. A German shepherd or a pit bull. Anything that's ready to tear the face off an intruder.

If I'm going to be a cowboy, I'll need a dog anyway. My own hound. All the cowboys in movies have dogs. He'll be my best friend since I'll be all alone up in God's country.

Between an angry dog and my gun collection, I should be okay.

At least, I can hope.

"That's gross." Lindy hops out of my truck once I turn off the ignition. "You can't just let it poop all over the yard! I'll never go to another one of your barbeques again."

Let's hope I make it to summertime so I can host another one of those said barbeques.

"Lindy, I brought you here to help me pick one out." And also because I don't want you wandering around by yourself in case someone decides to snatch you to get to *me*.

If I could've come up with a good enough excuse, I'd be carting Mom and Dad along with me, too. I've already seen first-hand what the Cinque family will do to anyone who fucks with them. And if you have loved ones?

I let out a shaky breath.

Lock them up, because nobody is safe.

They don't just stop with the target. They take out *everyone*.

We walk to the front door and pull it open. A bell chimes overhead, but nobody comes running. I hear a lot of barking — deep and menacing, shrill and high-pitched.

I'll take deep and menacing any day of the week, thank you.

Lindy claps her hands together. "You know what kind of dog you should get? A lab! They're so sweet and friendly!"

"Yeah, sweet and friendly isn't really on my list of dog selection criteria. I'm looking for one that's a little more…deadly."

Lindy furrows her brow. "What the heck for? I thought you just wanted a companion. Not that you don't have enough of the female human variety," she says in a sly voice, poking me in the side.

"Whoa, whoa, now," I say holding up my hands. "I don't talk to you about your…you know…stuff, and mine sure as hell isn't up for discussion. You're my baby sister, for Christ's sake."

Lindy giggles. "Don't worry. I wasn't offering to tell you about my…" she clears her throat. "*Stuff.*"

"Thank fuck for that." I tap the top of my sneaker on the shiny floor tile and look around. "Is there anyone here besides the animals?" I peek down the hallway, but there's no sign of a person. Just a lot of yappy dogs competing for air time. There's a bell hidden behind a plant on the desk, and I smash my hand on it.

I finally hear footsteps.

*Click, click, click.*

I roll my eyes, drumming my fingertips on the desk, when the clicking gets louder. Before the person appears, I let out a frustrated sigh. "You know, we're here to help an animal in need. Would be nice to—"

My breath hitches as a pair of ice-blue eyes sear through me.

Oh, Christ. I've fantasized about those eyes…and everything else that comes along with the package standing in front of me.

"It's hard to pull yourself away from a pack of hungry male dogs when they're eating lunch." Katarina Ivanov cocks an eyebrow and flashes a smirk at Lindy. "You know how men get when they're hungry."

Lindy giggles and nudges me. "Do I ever!"

"Kat?" I sputter the question because I'm so shocked right now that I could swear my eyes are deceiving me and the gorgeous Russian mafia princess isn't really standing before me in her signature six-inch high heels.

She folds her arms over her shirt, forcing her tits closer to the dangerously low neckline. "In the flesh."

Fuck me, did she really need to say flesh? Like I need any more encouragement.

"What the hell are you doing here?"

"I take care of the animals."

"How?" I exclaim. "By beating them senseless if they don't behave themselves?"

Lindy gasps and elbows me in the ribs.

Kat smirks. "I volunteer here. I love animals, but my work schedule doesn't allow for me to keep one. So I get my fix while I'm here."

My mouth is still hanging open. Who the fuck would have ever thought that Katarina was a philanthropist? I mean, yeah, she helps people...helps them meet their Makers, that is.

Lindy's eyes are still on Kat's. "Are you a model?" she blurts.

Kat shakes her head. "No."

"Oh, um, I just assumed, because I mean, you're beautiful and obviously know fashion. I love your boots," Lindy gushes.

"Thank you," Kat replies in her usual clipped voice. I still don't get how she has this job. People with black hearts and poison running through their veins aren't really the type you'd expect to see doing good for the sake of doing good.

Not that it changes the fact that I still have a hard-on for this woman, lethal or not.

"So what do you do?" Lindy presses. I turn a questioning gaze to my sister. Why the hell is she so interested, anyway? And is Kat going to tell her—?

"I'm a relationship manager for my father's businesses." Kat smiles, and I get the hint that the career conversation is now over. "So, *Rocco*," Kat says inching toward me. "What brings you here?"

I can see Lindy's gaze shoot from me to Kat and then back

again out of the corner of my eye. It's pretty damn clear that there will be plenty of questions pelted at me later about this little exchange.

I straighten and puff out my chest a little and fuck me if her lips don't curl into a tiny smile. "I'm looking for a dog."

"Why come here? Why not go to a breeder? These dogs need a lot of love and care. A lot of them have been beaten, tortured, and hurt really badly. They have a hard time trusting people." She creeps closer still. "What makes you think you can handle that kind of responsibility?"

I'm rooted to the spot. Her eyes lock on me, searching for something...maybe a reason to trust that I can do good, that I'm not all smoke and mirrors. Wow, she actually cares...about the animals. I never saw that one coming, the caring part.

She's one of the coldest people I've ever met.

Ironic that all that frigidness makes me hot as fuck.

"Look, Kat. I'm perfectly able to care for a damaged animal. I want to help one of them. I don't want some fancy purebred dog." I hope I sound as sincere as I think I do. Maybe there's a tiny part of me that wants her to be impressed that I want to do something good, that I'm not just some asshole thug who does nothing with his time except drink, maim, and fuck.

She nods her head, strands of her dark hair falling around her face. The rest of it is swept up onto the top of her head. Still glamorous, even when she cleans out animal cages. "And one other thing..." Kat's voice takes on a teasing tone. "How will you get the dog home? In your precious car? The one you don't allow people to sit in?"

Lindy lets out a loud chuckle. "Ha ha! Wow, do you ever have his number!" She pokes me again. "Rocco, tell her you brought the truck today!"

A surprised look crosses Kat's face. "So you're serious." She eyes me, her eyes raking me up and down just enough that I feel pleasantly violated. I can only imagine what she can do with her hands. "Okay, then. Let's go and meet some dogs. See if you can *connect.*" She puts extra stress on that word, her lingering glance making my dick twitch.

I'd like to show her all about how well I can connect...with *her*.

We follow Kat down a long hallway lined with cages. Her hips swing left and right with each step she takes in those sky-high heels. That ass. Good God, it's perfect. Tight, round, bitable. Christ, what I'd do to it if I had—

"How do you *know* her?" Lindy elbows me in the side and hisses in my ear. My baby sister is young and innocent. She doesn't need to be dragged into my work, which is why I never talk to her about it.

Or Kat, not that there's much there to talk about anyway.

Yeah, I fantasize about fucking Katarina six ways from Sunday, but that's my 'stuff' and I definitely don't talk to Lindy about that shit. Not now, not ever.

"She's a friend of Shaye's." All true. Lindy doesn't need the sordid details about how she's the daughter of a brutal Russian mob boss who pretty much owns the European drug trade. Or how I saved her life and shot some asshole who had a gun to her head...I don't remember getting a thank you for that, either.

Or the blow job I casually asked for.

"She's gorgeous!" Lindy says in a whisper-squeal. "You have to go out with her. I think she's into you."

"Easy, killer. Let's just do what we came to do, okay?"

"I'm just saying."

Kat stops at the far end of the hallway and turns back to us. "Are you looking for a big dog? A small one? Any specific type?"

"I want a big dog. A mean one."

Kat lifts an eyebrow. "You looking for protection, Rocco? Maybe a shelter isn't the best place for you. Maybe you should go and look at guard dogs instead." A tiny smile plays at her red lips.

Christ, I wanna bite them so bad...

I clear my throat. "That's not what I meant. I just want a strong personality. A dog who doesn't need to play all the time, since my work is pretty crazy, too. I need a dog that's okay on his own." I backpedal because the last thing I'm going to do is leave this place right now. In fact, I'm gonna milk this for all I can if it lets me hang out with Kat in a non-deadly situation where we can just talk and not have to fire guns to stay alive. Even on nights when we go out, we do it in a group, and it's after we've all been ass-rammed by her at poker. Seeing this human side is refreshing. I wonder what else she's hiding.

"*His* own?" Her lips twitch. "So I take it that means you associate a strong dog with a *male* dog, right? Because female dogs aren't as powerful?"

I let out a frustrated sigh. This woman. "Not what I meant. It just came out. If you have a female dog that is just as badass, I'm open to meeting her, too."

"Oh! Look at this one!" Lindy runs over to a large, dark brown dog with a gruff bark. It raises its eyes up at her, and Jesus...they look tired. And worn down. And defeated. The other dogs in here are pretty active and yappy, but not this one. It doesn't look like it can even be bothered to raise a paw in greeting. It looks like it just wants to be left alone.

Maybe being alone is better than what it experienced before it came here.

Maybe it just wants some peace and quiet.

I walk over to the cage. I can't explain it. I'm just drawn to this dog. I don't know if it's a male or a female, but I sense some kind of a connection. It's weird. I've never really been an animal person before, and I came here to find a dog the exact opposite of this one, but here I am, kneeling in front of the cage.

I hold out a hand and the dog drops its chin into it. Big brown eyes stare at me with a lot of questions, but there's only one I have the answer to.

This is the one.

Kat's heels click on the floor as they approach and she kneels next to me. "This is Stoli 2," she says, a smile lifting her lips as she reaches in to run her hand over the dog's dull coat. "It's a he, by the way."

I nod, still caught by his curious gaze. He still hasn't made a sound. "Does he bark?"

"He's kind of a quiet guy. But he'll chat when he's ready." She strokes the top of his head, and his eyes float closed. Yeah, you've got the life, Stoli 2. I'd love for her hands to be all over me, too.

"I'll take him." No hesitation. Somehow I know this is the dog for me. He's the guy I want next to me when I'm herding cattle upstate in New York.

A tiny pang in my chest reminds me that there are some bad people out to get me. Is it really fair to bring him into that?

Just one more thing to watch over and protect...

I rub my hand under his chin and he lets out a sigh. Maybe it's one of relief, maybe it's one of annoyance. I'm going with the first one, though.

"He's a special dog," Kat murmurs. "We've gotten to be good buddies, right?"

*Ruff!*

I grin. Of course he'd answer the beautiful woman. He ain't a stupid guy.

"Do you want to go home with Rocco?" she coos.

I furrow my brow and stare at her for a second until she meets my curious gaze.

"What are you looking at?"

My voice drops. "Sorry, it's just that I've seen you gouge out a guy's eye with a high heel. It's kind of a shock to see you like this, you know, and hear you talk like a human-type person."

She narrows her eyes, but she can't fight the smirk lifting her lips. "It'll be our little secret, okay?"

*Ruff! Ruff! Ruff!*

"He must like you." Kat straightens up. "He doesn't usually respond to people well. Or at all, really."

"Maybe it's you he's responding to."

She shrugs, but I can see a hint of sadness in her expression. "I think he'll be happy with you."

Stoli 2 is suddenly alive, his tongue hanging out of his mouth as he barks for Kat's attention. But she's somewhere else right now, and judging from her expression, it's not a happy place.

Yeah, I'd be sad to see her leave, too.

"Just give me a minute, and I'll grab the key." She backs away, dodging around Lindy where she's playing with some mutt.

Kat turns a corner and walks down a hallway, her shoulders hunched. I don't know why, but I race after her, leaving Lindy to monitor the animals. "Kat!" I call out. "Wait up!"

She stops short but doesn't turn around. I tumble into her, crashing us both into a wall with her body pressed against mine. I catch a whiff of some type of perfume. It's not some floral or fruity shit so many girls wear. It's classy. Sexy. Dangerous.

Well, it makes me want to do dangerous things.

Dangerously sexy things.

Oh, fuck me. I have to focus on something other than her tits rubbing against me. Maybe I should back away instead of plastering myself all over her against a wall with my sister only a few feet away.

My lips hover over hers, and all I want is one taste.

Then I realize her eyes are red and a little teary.

Another bit of human emotion. I didn't see that one coming either.

"What happened back there?" I murmur.

She shakes her head but says nothing.

Is she gonna cry? I don't know how to react if she cries. Jesus, I never even thought the woman had blood running through her veins. I always thought it was cyanide or some shit like that.

I knew how to deal with that Kat.

This version confuses me even more.

But it makes me want her more, too.

She blinks fast, her expression shifting before my thoughts finish running their course. "Is this how you get women to submit to you? By cornering them against a wall so they can't run away?" Her eyes take on a hard edge, and I feel a bit of relief flood over me.

The bitch is back.

I know how to deal with *her*.

"I've never had any complaints before. And I've got plenty of repeat customers." I wink and pull away, but that crackle of electricity still hums between us.

"You never did aim too high with your choices." Her eyes darken, and the jolt intensifies.

"I didn't know you were paying such close attention." My lips curl into a smirk, and a hint of pink spots her cheeks. Caught!

I knew she was watching. She's always watching. It's part of the reason why she's so damn good at her 'job' as a relationship manager.

"It's hard not to notice when a gaggle of mindless, shameless, yappy women *think* they've found their prize."

"What the hell is a gaggle?"

She rolls her eyes and pushes past me with a deep sigh.

"I'm kidding. But seriously, you give me a lot more credit than I deserve. I work with one or two at a time, tops. Never a whole gaggle." I chuckle. "Although, I'd be open to it."

Kat tucks a stray strand of hair back into the bun thing and swivels to face me. Any hint of emotion has been wiped away, leaving only her signature expression behind. It's so cold, I actually get a chill.

And it hits me right in the groin.

"Alexi! Bring me the key!" she calls out, her ice-blue eyes still focused on me. I'm caught. I can't break the spell...and I'm damn sure it's a spell she's cast on me, too. My limbs go numb, I can't think straight, and my dick twitches. That's about the only part of me that can function at all when she catches me in that penetrating gaze.

Penetrating.

Yeah...

I'm pretty sure she knows the effect it has on me, too. She loves the control. And this is only an example of what she can do with her *eyes*...

Fuck me.

I'd like to see more. Much more.

A loud thumping forces my attention away from Kat. I turn to see a tall guy stomping down the hall with a key ring dangling from one hand. He's taller than me and muscular, with light hair and eyes. And there's nothing friendly about him. He walks toward us, his heavy, black work boots thumping on the floor. His face is twisted into a grimace and his fiery glare is fixed right on me.

What the hell did I do to him?

Although...he looks kind of familiar.

Maybe there's a reason for the death look after all.

He hands her the keys without taking his eyes off of me. He says nothing, but then again, his menacing stare speaks volumes. I stretch myself to my full height, still falling short.

Way short. He's a goddamn giant. A Russian giant whose body has clearly responded well to all the bottles of vodka he's probably guzzled over the years.

Fucking scotch. I gotta make the switch to clear liquor.

"Who's this guy?" Alexi finally opens his mouth, his voice a low growl.

"Relax," Kat says, swinging the key ring around her finger. "He's a friend of Nico's. He's safe."

Safe. How hot is that?

I square my shoulders, thinking tall, hoping it adds the perception of some height. "Safe is not a word people would use to describe me."

"Sorry. I didn't know that word was so offensive."

"Just so we're clear. I am *very* dangerous." I eye Alexi and see his jaw twitch.

"Then we just might have a problem." Alexi steps closer to me and his voice drops even lower. How is that even possible?

"Enough, Alexi." Kat smirks at me. "Why is your voice so low all of a sudden?"

I narrow my eyes in response. "What are you talking about? This is my normal voice." It's not, but this guy hasn't heard me talk before. If I want to have any cred whatsoever, I need to make sure he knows I'm not *safe*.

"Mm-hm." She nods her head toward the area where the animal cages are kept. "Okay, both of you guys need to put away your dicks right now. Let's get Rocco all set up with his new friend."

I puff out my chest and follow Kat, pushing past Alexi. It's a risk, and I sure as hell hope he doesn't grab me by the neck and throw me against a wall.

He doesn't.

Thank fuck.

But then again, his attention is solely on Kat right now.

Are they together?

Shit.

I deflate a bit with that realization.

Kat rounds the corner, and I force my eyes away from her ass. If it belongs to someone else, there's no sense in fantasizing about it anymore.

She bends down and unlocks Stoli 2's cage. He's cautious, though. He steps onto the floor, one paw at a time. He doesn't rush anyone, but he does sit at Kat's feet.

Seems to be the common male reaction to this woman.

Complete and utter adoration for the master.

She reaches down and strokes the fur under his chin and his eyes float closed like there's nowhere else in the world he'd rather be.

If I were down there, I might feel the same way.

"I think he's going to be sad to leave you," Lindy says, still sitting in front of another cage.

"It's time for him to go home." Kat's eyes flicker over to me, and there's a very thinly veiled threat pretty apparent in her stare. "You'd better be good to him."

"I will..." I clear my throat and start again, remembering Alexi is still lurking. "I will make sure he is taken care of."

Lindy furrows her brow. "What's up with your voice?"

Kat stifles a snicker with her hand and heads toward the office up front. Alexi is right on her ass. But he gives me a long, threatening look before he follows her. I let out a deep sigh and help my sister up, following the caravan to the office to sign whatever paperwork I need to make Stoli 2 my own.

"Who's the tall dude?" Lindy whispers. "He's hot, but super scary."

"I don't know. Maybe her boyfriend."

Lindy gasps. "Oh no, really? I can't believe it! I'm never wrong with that stuff."

We walk into the office, and Alexi narrows his eyes at me when Kat leans over to show me everything I have to sign to take ownership of Stoli 2. I breathe in deeply; she's close enough that the loose strands of hair around her face graze my cheek.

He's watching, and I don't really give a fuck. I haven't laid a finger on her, and anything I do to her is solely in my mind.

He can try to kill me with his glare, but my mind is my own. If I want to screw his girl upside down in my fantasies, tough shit. He can't intimidate me. His voice may be deeper, but I'm basically staring death in the face.

I'm getting off one way or another.

"This is where you put his name," she says, pointing to a place on the form. I missed most of what she just said, but at least I'm with her on this one. I scribble Stoli 2 Lucchese on the form, and she lets out a soft chuckle. "You're keeping my name?"

"Yeah." I grin. "It suits him."

She nods and the sadness I caught earlier is back. It's only visible when she allows it to be, and for some reason, she wants me to see it. "You have no idea."

My mouth opens, and I try to think of something to say.

Lindy and Alexi are still here, so is Stoli 2. But Kat and I are in our own world right now, oblivious to everyone else. If I didn't know better, I'd swear this was Kat's twin sister because all of the vulnerability is throwing me for a loop. Still hot as fuck, but this version of her seems to feel.

"You can visit him anytime you want," I blurt out, catching Alexi's jaw twitch out of the corner of my eye. "I bet he'd love that."

Her smile fades, her hand dropping to Stoli 2's head. "Thanks, but sometimes you just have to say goodbye."

"That's fucking dismal."

"It's life."

There's so much I want to ask, so much I need to know.

I thought I wanted this girl before but seeing this side of her...the one that actually cares, the one that experiences pain and loss...I just want to pull her close and hold her without the risk of a deadly chokehold looming. It's like she's a superhero or something. In human form, she's like one of us. But when she's in kill mode, she takes on a completely different façade, one that's impervious to emotion.

She pulls away, and I feel the loss.

Stoli 2 rests his head on the top of my sneakers.

I guess he does, too.

Looks like we're gonna muddle through this together.

Once I finish the paperwork, I slide my chair back and stand up. "Thanks, Kat," I say, realizing I forgot to drop my voice. Dammit.

A tight smile stretches across her face. "Be good to him."

I nod, fighting the urge to punch the smug ass grin off of Alexi's face. "I'll see you around."

Lindy and I walk out of the shelter with Stoli 2, and I fling an arm across my sister's midsection, preventing her from moving forward. Not until I take in the sights. I check left and right before removing my arm.

"Rocco, what's up with you today? You're so jittery. And you kind of screwed up with Kat in there, too. Just saying. You losing your edge?"

I pull open the door to let Lindy in and then run around to the driver's side. Another all-over check confirms there aren't any people in sight, just cars zooming up and down the street. But there's a heaviness in my chest, some sick feeling that I'm missing something.

I shake my head and hop into the truck. "She's not interested, Lindy. Drop it, okay?"

"I'm just saying it looked like she was hot for *you*, not the Russian."

*Ruff! Ruff!*

Lindy giggles. "That's right, Stoli 2. Tell him we like Kat and we want her!"

I turn on the ignition and merge onto the road.

I want her, too.

But thanks to the Salesis, I know too much.

Too many things that would hurt her.

Or worse. Much fucking worse.

I can't say anything.

I can't give her what she wants…what I know she needs.

She's never spoken the words, but I've seen glimpses of her pain.

I could have helped her heal.

But I made my bed. Sealed my romantic fate.

I chose the family.

## Chapter Five
# KATARINA

*C*rack!
Tears stream down my cheeks as the target dances around in my view. Bullet holes pepper the cardboard cutout, but it's still not enough. It's barely recognizable anymore, but still I continue my assault on it.

It's not completely destroyed yet, like me.

*Pop! Pop! Pop!*

Rocco didn't know. I can't be mad about him adopting Stoli 2.

The ache in my chest is so damn heavy and firing off these bullets isn't making it any better. I plug the target with more holes, letting the grief and guilt guide my trigger finger. The bullets fly through the air, tearing through the cardboard. At least something is more broken and shredded than I am.

Ha! What a joke. It's completely whole compared to me.

And this little shooting spree doesn't change a thing.

I try to steady my breathing, but my heart thumps harder and harder as the seconds pass.

He wasn't mine. He was never mine. I lost my Stoli.

*Pop! Crack! Crack!*

Dammit, I'm such a fucking mess! Why is it such a surprise

to me after all this time? I know what's coming...I can feel the impending dread deep in my bones as the date approaches, but somehow I'm always shocked by it.

The nightmares are back. They haunt me each time I close my eyes. Nothing keeps the demons away while I sleep. They want me to remember, to relive that day over and over, to ignite the rage.

No amount of vodka mutes the chilling sounds or blunts the harsh reality I survived.

The horror of those memories...the screams, pleas for mercy, cries for help...I can hear the sounds all so clearly, almost as if I'm standing in our old kitchen again, watching my mother and sister struggle for their lives.

And for what?

Revenge. It's always about revenge.

I just need to dig a little deeper to figure out who needed revenge so badly that they had to destroy so much of what I loved about living.

I try in vain to fill the gaping void, but nothing works. Stoli 2 was temporary. It's all temporary. Letting myself care about something too much for too long...I can't do it. It hurts so badly, and I always seem to lose in the end.

That makes me angry. Very fucking angry.

*Crack! Crack!*

And the one person who can drag me out of this downward spiral won't let me in. For eight years, I've been hanging around on the outside, hoping for a glimpse of the father who evidently died with my mother and sister.

I have nothing, and the emptiness is like a black hole. I've been battling it for the past eight years, dancing around the edge, trying not to get sucked into it.

I want to forget. I want to live again.

But the anger won't let me.

So I close myself off and keep my distance. Nobody else

needs to be dragged into my toxic aura. It's pure poison for anyone who gets too close.

But one person can't take a hint.

Deep breaths. Focus, focus, focus. I squeeze my eyes shut and grip the gun tight in my hand. Rocco's face flashes across my mind, making me swallow hard. I grit my teeth. Fuck! I can't do this right now!

Forget about how close he was to my lips...how good he smelled...how fucking demented I am for even giving these thoughts air time.

He saved my life once before.

I let my guard down for a split second, and he rescued me.

He risked his own ass and didn't think twice about it.

Part of me wishes he hadn't.

Part of me wants the pain and loneliness to end.

The bigger part of me feels more for him than I should. The tangle of warmth in my belly when he smiles at me, the chills that shimmy down my spine when he's near, the urge to fling myself into his strong arms and bury my head in his cologne-scented neck with the hope to forget, if just for a little while—I feel it all.

So today at the shelter, I let him in, just for a second, just to see if he felt the same way.

I saw the need in his expression, felt the heat in his gaze. He's fucked me with his eyes more times than I can count, but today? Today he showed me more than I'd expected. Much more.

But emotions are too dangerous. They fuck with the mind and make you do stupid shit that gets people hurt or killed.

I already have plenty of blood on my hands.

I don't need his.

So I made a decision. I kicked him out and slammed the door shut.

*Crack! Crack! Crack!*

I can't give myself to someone if I'm only tiny shards of the person I used to be. That girl was awesome. She had a future. She had the love of her family. She was going places.

And I don't mean to shitty neighborhoods where she takes out bad guys who fuck with her livelihood.

I put the gun down on a table, clutch the sides of my head, and let out a bloodcurdling scream that could probably shatter the glass in here if it wasn't tempered.

Goddammit! I want to hurt someone! I want to inflict the same kind of burning, searing pain that slices through me, the type of pain you never forget because it cuts so deep and so hard and leaves a deep scar. I want someone to suffer the way I did!

The way I still do...

I need to find out the truth.

And then?

I torture the bastards who yanked everything away from me.

I make them pay.

## Chapter Six

# ROCCO

"It's been days. When the hell are you gonna fill me in?"

"Soon." Nico's gaze darts left and right while we stand at the bar of Culaccino II, the sister nightclub Max runs for Nico. He's clearly looking for any excuse to get away from me. He's been avoiding my calls and texts, and I'd just like to know why.

Why, goddammit?

Maybe it means that the Cinques are about to put the drop on me, and he's given up trying to save my ass.

That's a pleasant thought.

"Listen," I say, my voice dropping. "You know something is up. I can tell. I don't know what the fuck horses have to do with the Cinques, but there's obviously some connection. How much longer are you gonna make me wait?"

"I'm still working on it."

"Nico, the Cinques just tried to take down our family in a pretty big way. They spent a lot of money and put a lot of trust in those idiot Bonnaro brothers to get the job done. It was an epic fucking fail. You think they're gonna just sit back and sun their asses in California while snacking on wheatgrass or avocado toast or whatever the fuck else shit they eat out there? Hell no!

They're coming, Nico. They're coming for me. And if Kat finds out—"

His eyes narrow, his mouth stretching into a tight line. "But she won't, right, Rocco? She won't find out because that was part of the deal."

I grit my teeth. "I'm not saying she'd find out from me."

"Then what are you saying? That she'd somehow miraculously find evidence of what really happened the day her family was butchered and connect all the dots?"

"It could happen."

"No, actually, it couldn't. Not unless someone connects them for her." He pokes me in the chest. "And that would be deadly. For both of you."

She doesn't know what I know. Hell, she's never told me a damn thing about her past. But I've heard it all and seen plenty.

They told me they'd kill me if I breathed a word of it to her.

Which was fine, until I started to like her. Like her in a way that would put me six feet under if her father ever read my mind and saw her in some pretty damn compromising positions.

The woman with ice for blood and a body that can shame a porn star.

Fuck, yeah, I liked her.

But after today at the animal shelter?

I realized that 'like' had taken a different turn, a very unexpected one.

'Like' had turned into something else, something deeper, something that scares the crap out of me.

And now all I want to do is protect her.

It's bad enough knowing that I have to cover my own ass. But Kat...who the fuck is covering hers? Because these people... they don't stop. They sit back, take deep breaths, sometimes very fucking long ones...eight years long...but they always jump back into the flames. The hell they created.

Sometimes I think death is more rewarding to the Cinque family than money.

I saw that firsthand when I became one of them...under false pretenses.

"Hey! Where the hell have you assholes been?" Max swoops in, clapping both of us on the backs. "It's opening night! You should have been here with a bottle of champagne hours ago to help me celebrate!"

"Don't worry about it. We've got plenty of time for that." Nico smirks, looking everywhere but in my direction. "Place looks good. Nice work."

"Thanks." Max nudges me. "Hey, I left you a bunch of messages. What the hell?"

I rub the stress knot in the back of my skull. "Sorry, I've been busy."

"Busy with what? Playing with yourself? I could've used some help preparing the place for tonight."

Nico's head twists back and he pins me to the wall with a threatening glare. As if I'm gonna fuck up and say shit that I know I'm not supposed to...shit that can fuck all of us up pretty bad.

And I thought the blow-out we had a month ago with the Bonnaro family was bad. They'd partnered with the Cinques to take down our family in an elaborate sex and drug trafficking scheme, inflicting a little vengeance for us working with Viktor Ivanov, their sworn enemy. They would have succeeded, too, if Nico hadn't taken control of the situation and sent in a mole to figure out their plans ahead of time. He's always ten steps ahead of everyone, which should make me feel a little bit better about what's going to happen.

It doesn't.

Because I know what can happen if shit goes sideways.

*When* shit goes sideways.

It always does, no matter how much or how long we prepare.

That's pretty much a guarantee.

Nico pulls his phone from his pocket and stares at it. "Guys, I'll catch up with you later. I need to take care of something." He gives me one last hard look before disappearing into the crowd of drunk ass people grinding around us.

Max smirks at me. "So do you know what's up his ass these days? I mean, he should be relaxing since the Cinques are coming after you and not him, right?"

"Thanks, dick." I rub the knot again, but it's even tighter now. How is that even possible?

"Listen, you know I have your back. Although, it was pretty damn stupid of you to screw around with one of their women, then cut and run. You fuck one of them, and then all of them fuck *you*."

"Thanks for reminding me." Yeah, it wasn't my brightest move. And it's the only thing Max knows about my time in California. Nobody except my dad, Viktor, and Nico know what I was really doing and why I was really doing her.

I needed to get close, and Daniela Cinque was my one sexy, leather-clad roadblock to finding out the truth. I had to break into her business and fucking her was the only way inside.

Unfortunately for me, it turns out she's more dangerous than the men in that family.

And I feel the noose tighten around my neck constantly even though she's out in Los Angeles, and I'm in New Jersey.

I knew I wouldn't be able to hide out for too long. When I came back here, Nico made sure I was in jobs where his security could keep an eye on me. And for some reason, the Cinque family has let me live.

That makes me very nervous. The longer they keep me alive, the worse my ending will be.

I'm tired of looking over my shoulder.

I just want a normal life, is that so much to ask for? I'm not a bad person, but somehow I end up doing a lot of bad shit for good reasons.

"How much longer do you think—?"

I shake my head. "Don't even say it."

"You managed to escape them for this long. Maybe they'll

leave you alone. Maybe they have bigger things to deal with. Why bother with your sorry ass? So you fucked around with Daniela. I'm sure she's had better since then."

I roll my eyes. "Screw you."

Max snickers. "Don't be so sensitive. I always knew that was why you lifted so much. Compensating for a small cock. That's why you're still alive. Daniela probably feels sorry for you and your little dick. Figured it wasn't worth the effort of killing you."

"You're a real tool."

"I know I *have* a real tool, unlike you, bro." Max nudges me. "Come on, you need another drink. Lemme buy you one."

I stare into my empty glass and jiggle the ice cubes around. He's right. I definitely need more booze to work through the shit going on in my head right now. I follow Max to the bar. I like this new version of him. He's in love, has his own club...he's a changed man. Completely opposite of the borderline psycho he used to be, although I do miss that lunatic sometimes. He was an entertaining bastard to watch.

I put my glass on the bar and Max orders two scotches. "Wait," I say. "I'll have a Stoli on the rocks. Make it a double." In honor of my new pal, Stoli 2.

And Kat.

Is it weird that having the dog makes me feel closer to her?

Christ, this stress is making me feel shit that's completely foreign.

The bartender slides the glass of clear liquid in front of me, and I take a long gulp. The vodka burns a path down my throat. Pure rubbing alcohol. It may be smooth, but that part escapes me as I choke it down.

Max claps me on the back. "Hey, have as many as you want and put everything on my tab. I'm gonna find Sloane."

I nod and hold up my glass. "I'll just be here."

Max walks toward a corner and dips his head down to give his girlfriend Sloane a kiss. I shake my head, still wondering how Max of all people would fall for a good girl like her. His dick was always wrapped up in girls who owned more clothes made of pleather and lace than cotton, whose faces were masks of makeup, and who choked on three-syllable words.

Sloane, though...she really turned him inside out. And I'm happy for him. For them.

It's taken him a long time to forgive me for what I did to him years ago, but I'm glad it finally happened.

And he doesn't even know the truth.

I see Nico sink down next to his girlfriend Shaye, Max's sister and Sloane's best friend. He drapes an arm over her shoulders and she smiles up at him. I have no doubt that's the thing he had to 'take care of' before.

That's just great.

Everyone is fucking happy.

I'm so glad for all of them.

And I'm the only asshole who's left dodging death.

I take another long gulp of my vodka and swing myself around to face the bar. I slam my near-empty glass on the dark wood and drop my head into my hands.

"Rough night?"

I peek through my fingers, dragging my hand down the front of my face. I manage a half-grin. "So rough I needed vodka."

Kat smiles. "I always told you it makes things better. Fuck the scotch. Shoot the vodka instead."

*Shoot it, lick it off your tits...I'll do anything you want with it.*

"I didn't think I'd see you tonight."

She lifts an eyebrow. "So you thought about seeing me?"

I run a hand through my hair and look away since my poker face is shit when she's around. "I wondered who'd show up. It's not like I thought about you specifically."

"Mm-hm." Her red lips curl upward, and it's hard for me to not think about them sucking my cock and leaving her mark on me.

I clear my throat. "So Stoli 2, he's, uh, a really good dog.

Lindy wanted to stay with him tonight, so I brought him over to my parents' house. Thought he'd like the company."

"He was..." she murmurs, a faraway look in her eyes. I wish I knew where she was right now.

Something tells me I already do know, and there's not a damn thing I can do about it unless I have a death wish.

But as quickly as the look appeared, it's gone, and her eyes are all boarded up again.

"You know, you can come by and see him whenever you want." I don't know why I feel the need to make this offer again, but she's with me right now. She doesn't have to be. She could have found Shaye and the rest of the crew who are already here in the club, and let's face it...

We've always had kind of a lust-hate relationship.

Okay, maybe the lust thing is a little one-sided.

*My* side.

She's not running, though. She's right next to me.

And there's definitely something weighing on her mind.

"Thanks." Her smile fades, and she taps her long fingernails on the bar.

"So where's Alexi?" I narrow my eyes behind her, but I don't see the beefy Russian anywhere near her.

"I came by myself. I wanted to be alone."

I scrub a hand down the front of my face. "You wanted to be alone *here*? On opening night?" I know I'm a guy and I miss a lot, but this shit is confusing. Is she speaking girl code right now? Or is it that I had two doubles too many to be able to process her words?

She shrugs and gulps her shot. Not even a flinch. It *has* to burn, but you'd never know it by looking at her. Jesus, she's sexy as fuck.

"Max is my friend, and I wanted to be here for him. I just didn't want any...baggage."

I let out a snort and pick up another full shot. "You call your boyfriend baggage, huh? Maybe it's time to cut that shit off, yeah?"

She lifts an eyebrow and watches me gulp the shot. "Who said he's my boyfriend?"

"Seems like you can't go ten feet without him on your ass lately."

"Seems like you've been paying pretty close attention to my ass lately." She picks up another shot and holds it to her deep red lips. "And if he was my boyfriend, what difference would it make to you?"

Oh, Christ, that's a loaded question. "He's an arrogant prick."

"You think an arrogant prick would be bad for me?" She inches closer, the heat of her breath singeing my skin. Tiny hairs on the back of my neck stand at attention, even though this place is hot as hell. I fist my hands, fighting the urge to grip her slim hips and pull her against me. I want to taste so badly, and she knows it. I can see it in her eyes. She's taunting me, daring me to make a move.

Or maybe I'm just really drunk, and I'm making all of this shit up in my head.

"I think *that* arrogant prick has no idea how to handle you."

"Maybe I don't like to be handled. Maybe I like to be the one handling," she breathes against my ear.

My mouth drops open, but no words come out.

For a second, I thought she was going to try the human thing out again.

But, no. She's back to her tried and true fembot ways. Using sex as a diversion while she grabs control over the poor sucker caught in her trap.

I'm completely blank.

I have nothing.

She pulls away, a smirk tugging at her lips. She got what she came for, and now she's gonna leave me with these aching fucking blue balls.

The woman is ruthless.

At least I know why she came to find me first.

She pushes past me and walks toward the table in the back, her hips swinging with each step she takes. I watch her tight body weave through the crowd, and I don't even try to hide it when she looks back at me with a knowing smile.

Fuck it. I smile back.

Even though I'm already in deep with no lifeline in sight, I can't help myself.

I want her.

And I may be the only one who can protect her.

## Chapter Seven

# KATARINA

"Rocco is over there giving you such an eye-raping right now!" Shaye lets out a loud snort and falls over on the couch. "Are you sore, Kat?"

I smirk at Nico. "Wow, it sure doesn't look like you're going to be doing anything fun in the bedroom tonight." I nod at Shaye who's still lying flat on her back on the couch, chuckling at her mostly accurate observation. "I think you'll be spending it in the bathroom holding back your girlfriend's hair."

Nico groans. "She can't hold her liquor at all."

"In my defense, I only had a bowl of cereal today." Shaye swings herself to a sitting position and points to me. "What did you eat?"

"A fifth of vodka." I smirk. It's in my blood, what can I say?

Sloane, Shaye's best friend, giggles. She picks up a bottle of water. "Ugh, I can't even stomach the thought of vodka."

"Where's the man of the hour? Making the rounds?" I ask Sloane.

A deep pink flush creeps into her cheeks, and her eyes glow like candles at the mention of Max. "Yes. He keeps coming over to check on me, but I told him not to worry." She winks at Shaye. "Since *I'm* the sober one here."

Nico pours a shot of Belvedere vodka, and I scrunch up my nose when he hands it to me. "Seriously? I'm not drinking that shit. Get me something else."

He sees Max pass by our booth. "Hey, do you have any speed rack vodka you can bring over for Kat? She's making faces at your good booze."

"She's-s loyal, Nico. You've gotta respect that," Shaye slurs, her head rolling back against the cushion.

Fucking A right. I'm loyal with a capital L.

Max brings over a bottle of Stoli and sets it in front of me with a wink. "If the lady wants speed rack, she gets speed rack."

I laugh and swat his arm after the bottle is safely in my grasp. "Thanks."

I pour myself a drink and take a sip. My eyes wander back to the bar where I found Rocco earlier. My gut twists a bit when I see the now-empty area where I'd left him. I twist a strand of my hair around my finger, scouting the rest of the club. I bite down on my lower lip. Would he have left? Without saying goodbye? Without trying to—?

Sonofabitch!

*Why* would he even try? I shut him down every chance I get.

Is it because of my sick need for control?

Or is it because I'm afraid that I'll fall for him if I don't?

I drain the rest of my glass, half-listening to the conversation around me. Who the hell knew that I'd ever end up as part of this group? After the attack on our family, Papa let me in on some things...plans he had to crush his enemies and expand his interests here in America. He blamed himself for the deaths of Mom and Lili, not that he ever said as much. But once they were gone, he made sure he was glued to my side. If ever he took a business trip, he brought me along. I'd hoped it would make us closer, make him remember how it was to be a father. But being so close physically did nothing for my heart and soul. The emptiness always remained.

Maybe carting me around eased his guilt, but it only made

me feel more and more alone. He barely talked, never spoke about that day. He never asked me how I felt, if I missed them, if I was hurting, if I wanted to talk about things.

He completely iced over. All of his emotions froze, just like his heart.

I no longer had a family.

*But I didn't die with them! I'm still here, and he doesn't care!*

I'm an asset to the family. I'm a trained lethal weapon. I'm a trusted confidante.

But deep down, I'm also still that petrified sixteen-year-old girl who's crouched behind the kitchen island watching her mother get bludgeoned with a Ming vase and her sister get brutally raped.

I'm still the scared kid who has nobody to talk to, nobody to cry with, nobody to hug.

Sometimes I wish they'd killed me, too.

Living alone in this empty shell hurts worse than any pain those bastards could have inflicted.

The person who is supposed to be closest to me is the one who treats me like a stranger. He wants me to carry on the family business but snaps when I try to make him proud. Or happy. Or something other than the cold and stoic asshole he's become.

For years, I'd lived in Lili's shadow. She was always a better gymnast, a better student, more dependable, more sensitive to people's feelings...things that never really mattered much to me. I was always the rogue, the one who would sneak out in the middle of the night to go to parties, the one who studied five minutes before a test, the one who got sent to detention for making out with my boyfriend, Remy, in the boys' locker room.

Sometimes I feel like that shadow is still hanging over me, except the stakes are higher and my aversion to authority has only gotten stronger.

It should have been me and not Lili.

I wiggle my toes in my new Jimmy Choo booties and take

another sip of vodka. I don't even know how much I've had. Today, tonight, the hours seem to blend together. I drink it like water, and it numbs the pain that slices through me after every conversation I have with Papa.

Today was bad. And tomorrow...tomorrow will be horrible.

It always is.

That's really why I came here. I needed to forget, at least for a little while. I needed to ditch my past...and Alexi...for my future.

Whatever the hell will come of it. From day to day, I just never know.

I don't trust easily. Alexi is my only real friend. He knows more about me than anyone. He knows me better than my own father, for Christ's sake. And Rocco is right. Alexi has been all over me like maggots on rotting meat since that conversation with Papa. I've gotten no less than thirty texts from him since lunchtime, just checking in. He also showed up at my place, but I managed to convince him I was staying in. Showing up to the door in my robe with my hair piled on my head gave him peace of mind, I suppose, and he finally left me alone for the night.

But I don't need protection. I want to be exposed and appear vulnerable. Maybe it'll bring the demons out to play.

I have some games in mind...

And the people sitting around me right now...I know I can count on them. They'd have my back. They've proven it before.

How ironic that they don't know me at all.

Maybe if they did, they wouldn't be so willing to help me.

I take another gulp of my drink and twist away from their laughter. I take in a sharp breath, my heart thumping. If I'd have just waited a split second longer, I wouldn't have seen it. And fuck me, I wish I hadn't.

Because one person has claimed a place in my otherwise dismal future, the one who keeps creeping into my thoughts, who has me fantasizing like a teenaged girl mooning over the newest boy band sensation.

And he has not one, but two slutty bitches draped all over him.

"Ohh. Would you look at that?" Shaye leans over, her hair spilling into my glass. I pull it away so she doesn't knock it out of my hand.

"What are you talking about?"

She points in Rocco's general area. I say general because her hand is waving around like she's signing her name in the air. "That."

I shrug. "He can dance with whomever he wants to. Good for him, you know?"

"You're mad, Kat. I can tell. Why don't you go over there and kick their whorey asses-s?" She giggles, pulling herself onto her knees. "You know you want to," she taunts. "And you know you can."

I glance back at the girls. Of course I *can*. That's not even a question.

But kicking their asses wouldn't make me happy.

Kicking *his* would.

He did this to me! He turned me inside out! I was perfectly content with my empty and meaningless life, daily battles with underworld scumbags topped off with a boatload of regret and guilt eating away at me.

At least I had Stoli 2.

But now I have nothing.

And I want *something*, goddammit!

I jump to my feet and slam my glass on the table.

Shaye snickers. "You can't even help yourself, can you? You're such a badass-s, Kat."

A head case is more like it.

"Go get him," she hisses. "Make him realize what he's-s missing!"

I run a hand through my long dark hair and look down at her. Glassy eyes, flushed cheeks, and mussed hair. She's hammered beyond belief, but even she can see through me.

That cannot happen.

I never show my hand.

Ever!

I push through the sweaty crowd, my ass and tits being groped every step of the way. I don't even bother to acknowledge the hands...or their owners. Any other time, I'd have laid out each and every one of these handsy jerkoffs, listening to them cry about broken wrists and fingers.

But tonight, they lucked out. I don't stop. I don't make eye contact. I don't utter a single word.

Not until I get to my destination.

My pulse throbs against my neck as I close the space between us. I approach him from behind, peeling one of Bitch #1's hands off of his back. I lace his fingers with my own and slide his palm over my hip, just before I push Bitch #2 out of her position next to him. I don't speak, I just inch closer. I look up at him through half-hooded eyes. His other hand is around my waist now, gripping me tight.

My lips curl upward. The look of shock on his face is quickly replaced with one of pure, carnal lust. A tingling sensation deep in my belly forces me closer still, until my body is pressed against him. His cock thickens against me and my pussy clenches. I drag my fingernails down the sides of his torso, leaning my head back so I can feel his smoldering gaze melt me from the inside out.

Control, control, control.

It's completely lost.

His lips crush against mine, his hands fisting my hair. Tongues coiling, teeth cracking, mouths feasting...oh God, I need this. His hands move from my hair to my ass. He backs me into a corner, pressing me against a column in the darkness. Strobe lights flash in front of my eyes, temporarily blinding me. But when my vision clears, I can see the need in his heated gaze. The desire. The ache.

I feel all of it, too.

I pull him close, devouring his lips like a starved woman

desperate for sustenance. His hands run up and down my sides, grazing my breasts, and I have the sudden urge to fling a leg around his waist.

Right here in the open.

Because at this second, I need to let go of everything.

I want to come undone just once, to get the hell out of my head and let myself really feel.

Just for a little while.

I want to live.

I want a glimpse of what could have been if I was anyone other than me, if things had been different, if they weren't so complicated.

I can't have normal.

And I sure as hell can't *be* normal.

But none of that matters now.

The ache is so deep, and only one person can take it all away.

Rocco pulls away, leaving me breathless.

Talk about blue bean.

"Kat," he pants. "What the fuck—?"

I grasp his belt and tug. "Do you want me, Rocco?"

His shoulders quake, his breathing still labored. But those eyes...they tell me everything I want to know.

I just need him to speak the words.

"Yeah," he rasps, snaking an arm around my waist. "I want you bad, Kat. But—"

I shake my head. "No buts."

"No buts, huh? Fuck me," A smirk lifts his deliciously swollen lips. "I was really hoping you were *that* girl."

I rub my hand over his jeans, cupping his hard cock over the denim.

He lets out a groan. "Christ, Kat...what the hell are we doing?"

"I know exactly what I'm doing," I murmur, tickling his ear with my tongue and teeth. "And I know exactly what I want to do."

"Kat, we can't..." He squeezes his eyes shut and rakes a hand through his hair. "We just can't."

I drop my hand, my jaw damn-near hitting the floor. "Are you kidding me right now? I'm throwing myself at you, and you're turning me down?"

"I just...it's not the best time, and—" He looks around, avoiding my eyes. "I don't want it to be like this." He turns back to me, eyes narrowed. "Besides, you didn't give a shit about this before you saw me with another girl."

"Two girls," I mutter, flipping my hair over my shoulder.

"Oh, right, sorry. Two girls." He shakes his head and backs away from me. "You know, you can't dick around with me one minute and then ignore me the next one. I'm not a fucking yo-yo."

"Sorry," I grumble. "So sensitive. I didn't realize you were *that* guy."

He shakes his head, his mouth...the one that was plastered against mine only seconds ago...is now twisted into a grimace. "Yeah, well, I guess I am." With a glare that extinguishes every last ember of desire flickering in my body, he stalks away without another word.

I watch him stalk to the back of the club, probably to find one or both of the bitches I sent packing. I clench my fists tight, my long fingernails digging into the flesh. It hurts at first, but I ignore the pain and I dig harder. I may even be drawing blood. I don't give a fuck.

My threshold for pain is pretty high. And after what I've been through?

It's going to take a hell of a lot more than a rejection from Rocco Lucchese to make me shed a tear.

The colored rays of light illuminate the dance floor. Everyone is dancing, smiling, and laughing. There's also a damn lot of PDA, some that should really be taken to a different location. Some people...and I can't exactly exclude myself based on the scene I just caused...just have no shame. And the rest of them? Hell, they're drunk off their asses and having a great time.

I've never felt so goddamn alone in my life.

My throat tightens. It was nice for those fleeting moments to have someone's arms around me, someone to take away the anger and fill the void. To feel wanted on a deeper level...it's what I crave...what I've been craving since I met Rocco.

I never cared about that before. Sex was a cold and temporary escape, a distraction from my quest for vengeance.

For so many years, my sole focus was finding the bastards who took the lives of Mom and Lili. The last relationship I had was with Remy eight years ago. Remy whom I never saw again after that fateful day.

Dad couldn't get away from that part of our lives fast enough.

So I never got to say goodbye.

The loose ends in my past...Christ, there are too many to count.

I pound my fists against the column behind me and storm over to the ladies' room to fix my lipstick. If I can't seduce Rocco, I'm sure I can find a suitable substitute.

Because tonight of all nights, I really don't want to be alone.

And if I can't unleash all of my deep-rooted anger and blow someone's brains out, I need to fuck them out of someone. After that blatant rejection, the need is even more pressing.

We each deal with the grief in our own unique way.

I eradicate the sadness by inflicting harm on others.

And Papa has his own sick tradition, one he'd never shared with me, but one I know of only through Alexi.

Maybe because it reminds him that I watched the horrors unfold without stopping any of it.

But the fact that he shared something so personal with someone other than me...dammit, it stings.

Really fucking badly.

Just one more source of rage to battle.

I pull open the door and walk into the darkened lounge. The

wall sconces give off a dim glow, and I blink back the tears for what seems like the millionth time this week. These emotions have taken hold and just will not let me go.

I need more vodka.

And then some cock.

A combination that makes everything better...numb, at least.

I run my fingers through my hair, combing through the knots caused by Rocco's demanding fingers...fingers I wish I'd felt in so many other places before he went and grew a vagina.

Fucking yo-yo...I'd like to string him up and show him what that would *really* feel like.

I swipe under my eyes and clean up my dark eyeliner. It makes my eyes look almost clear. Soulless. Like there's nothing to hide.

Ironic.

And quite the opposite.

The lounge door slams open and loud, obnoxious voices float over to the mirrored area where I'm fixing myself.

"...fucking whore...grabbed him...pushed me away...so hot...gone..."

The bitching is followed by a smattering of laughter and then the main grumbler starts in again.

"If I see her again, I'm gonna fuck her shit up!"

Yeah, that came across loud and clear. A tiny smile tugs at my lips as I swipe on some more lipstick and pucker for my reflection.

Oh, yes. Please, please, please! Make my fucking night!

The promise of a bitch brawl suddenly has me hotter than a stiff cock.

Why the hell is that? What in the hell is wrong with me?

I wait, my pulse thudding in my neck. Oh, the urge to pummel is so damn strong!

High heels click on the marble floor and stop suddenly. I bite the inside of my mouth, fighting back a surge of gleeful laughter.

Then I wait for what I know is coming.

Because bitches like that always get booze muscles. She probably took a self-defense class once and thinks she can bring me to my knees with one stupid sweep of her stick-like leg.

She may be tall, but if she attacks, she's damn stupid, too.

My fingers twitch as I toy with the lip gloss tube.

"Hey!"

And here it comes...

I ignore her, of course, and that pisses her off.

Makes her friends egg her on.

Oh, Christ, this gets me off.

"I'm talking to you, bitch!"

A fingernail pokes me in the back and my spine stiffens. I swear my nipples get hard at the very same second.

Jesus, do I have problems...

I turn around slowly, a tight smile on my face. "I believe there are more polite ways of getting someone's attention," I say with the most fake smile I can muster.

The girl takes a few very confident steps toward me, her hands on her hips. I lift a brow and eye her heels. She couldn't begin to imagine the damage I've done with stilettos like that in my sordid past.

Ignorance. It really *is* bliss.

"Nobody cockblocks me!" she shouts, flipping her hair over one bare shoulder. Extensions. Nice. I hope they're the kind that are glued to her hair because they're about to be ripped from her scalp.

My fingertips tingle, excitement coursing through me at what's to come.

I know, but they don't.

And when I'm finished here, I'm sure she'll remember her manners next time and accept defeat with a little more grace and self-respect.

I say nothing. She wants me to engage, but I just watch. The alcohol flooding her veins is making her angry, vicious, and impulsive.

Ha! That's *my* normal.

"Say something, you whore!" She closes the space between us, stumbling in heels she clearly wears only when she wants to get laid, and shoves me backward. But the force does nothing. My footing, unlike hers, is solid. Uncompromised.

But one push was all I needed. With one swift movement, I grab her wrist, flip her around so her back is against me, and hook my arm through hers. I apply pressure...just enough to make her yelp.

"You should be happy that all I did was cockblock you, sweetie."

"Fuck you!" she rasps, gritting her teeth.

The bitch brigade springs into action and her two friends are now on either side of me. They think since my hands are occupied that I can't possibly defend myself.

Fucking morons.

The girl wiggles against me, trying to break loose. I'm not even holding her that hard, but she's compromised right now and she can't do much except head butt me from behind.

It's not really working well for her.

The other two stand on either side of me, exchanging glances. They don't want to stand on the sidelines, but they clearly don't have any clue how to take me out.

The one on my right is edging closer. When she reaches for my hair, I whip out a hand and fling it back, crushing it against her nose. I fling the girl in my arms around so she's facing me and then I back her against the wall, my arm right under her chin.

"I don't think dipshit number three wants to make a move, am I right?" I turn my head toward the third girl whose eyes are bugging out of their sockets. She shakes her head without a word.

*Let her go, Kat. Let all of this anger go. Brutalizing this girl won't bring me back, and you know it.*

I wince, a sharp pain slicing at my insides. Sometimes I hear that voice...her voice...and wonder if she's taken over as my conscience. When she was alive, I'd hear it a lot more — her attempt at using twin mental telepathy to keep me on the straight and narrow.

It worked...sometimes.

I grit my teeth and loosen my grip.

While Thing 1 chokes out some more expletives, Thing 2 is busy blubbering about the fact that I've just ruined her new ten-thousand-dollar nose.

I grin. "It really wasn't worth ten grand. Maybe now you can get it done right." I remove my arm from the throat of my first assailant, and her hands fly up to her neck as she chokes and gasps for air.

"You're fucking crazy! You almost killed me!" she sputters.

I lean into her, pinning her to the wall with only my hard gaze. "Consider yourself lucky. I don't usually let people live to tell the story." I walk toward the door of the lounge, flexing my fingers.

She's still in one, albeit a little bruised, piece. I could have mangled the shit out of her and her friends, but I didn't. I listened...this time. Now I'm all alone again with a hell of a lot of pent-up rage surging through me.

*I hope you're happy, Lil.*

## Chapter Eight
# ROCCO

"You animal!" Max claps me on the back. "I saw you guys out there on the dance floor attacking each other. You need to close the deal? I can find you a place."

I rub the back of my neck. "I don't need a place. Nothing happened. Nothing's *gonna* happen."

"Why the hell would you say that? She was all over you, man. She wants the Italian sausage. What are you waiting for?"

"Look, it was a stupid thing to do. I can't..." I let out a frustrated sigh. I want to, so badly. But how can I? If she knew what I do...what I'm keeping from her, she'd slice my jugular and leave me for dead.

And if she didn't finish the job, her father would.

There's really no shortage of people who'd love to butcher me.

But Max doesn't know about any of it, other than I was a mole for the Salesi family. He has no clue about Kat's family. She never once offered an explanation about why it was just her and her dad showing up here in New Jersey, and people in this life know better than to ask questions.

"Before the Cinques come knocking, I think you should tap that. Don't waste any time. Let's face it, you don't know how much you have left." He nudges me and lets out a loud chuckle. "Don't shit your pants or anything, bro. You know I've got your back. I won't let anything happen to you. If those cocksuckers show up in our territory, I'll take out every last one."

"Easy. You've got a girlfriend now, remember? Big shot club owner? You've got shit to take care of."

"Hey." He shoves me backward so I have no choice but to look him straight in the eye. "*You're* part of the shit I need to take care of. I will never forget everything you did for me, Rocco. Never."

I nod and crack a smile. "So I guess I'm forgiven, huh?" I say, referring to our fallout…the one that changed my life forever…the one that sent me into the pits of hell, to witness shit I'd never in my life imagined, to find the other half of a woman who has me questioning a lot of shit about my life right now.

I screwed Max over, yeah. Hell, I've screwed a lot of people over in my life. Sometimes it was to carry out an order, and sometimes it was just the lesser of two evils. Max doesn't care why he got fucked over anymore. I think he's just happy that he's free from all of the shit that was weighing him down. He's calm…er, anyway. He used to be a crazed motherfucker who'd fly off the handle if you so much as rolled your eyes at him. Beware the baseball bat.

But he's a different person now, one I know I can count on, and one I thank God really does have my back.

Because when the Cinques do come calling, I know he'll be all over them like flies on shit. You can put a suit on the guy, but you can't cover the crazy forever. And I'm gonna need that crazy sometime soon.

I stare at my phone while Max keeps talking about…Christ, I don't even know. I stopped listening a few minutes ago. At least he's off the topic of Kat.

I still can't get her face out of my head…the shock, the anger, the rejection. I saw it all, and to be honest, it shocked the shit out of me. The girl has a better poker face than anyone I've ever met. It's how she manages to rape us every time we dare to play cards with her. She can't lose. She never shows any signs of defeat, even when she's holding a complete crap hand.

And shame on us assholes for not having learned her tricks.

But tonight, she showed me something I never in a million years expected...vulnerability. It's just too much. First, those moments at the shelter and now this.

La Femme Nikita doesn't have feelings. She doesn't have emotions, so how the fuck can she show them?

Right?

She's a killer and fucking fierce as they come.

Calculating, ruthless, cold...is it all a façade?

Because what I saw earlier...what I felt earlier...makes me think there's a hell of a lot more to this woman than I thought.

I never meant for this to happen. I never wanted to fall for her...especially after seeing her gouge out some guy's eyeball with a stiletto. Yeah, it turned me on, but it should have scared me even more.

I knew from the very beginning that I could never have her, that all of the lies would eventually crush me. And if they didn't, she definitely would.

Katarina Ivanov is dangerous, but her deadly wrath doesn't scare me nearly enough as the feelings she's stirred up inside of me.

That fury swirls around her like a toxic aura. It has the power to choke anyone who gets too close to her.

At least that's how she plays her role.

But I've seen another side...not once, but twice.

The side that feels. The side that's suffering. The side that's lost.

I caught those glimpses, and they only made me want her more.

But knowing that I could maybe make it better...that I could take away some of that pain...

It doesn't matter how much I ache for her. There was no way

I could give in to her, much as I wanted to. I can't make this any worse than it is.

I can't have her. I need to finish the job. I need to keep focused.

At least, that's what I keep telling myself.

I'm already in too deep, and let's face it. I'm on borrowed time. If Kat finds out the truth about what I've done...

I give my head a little shake.

Christ, I hope the truth sets *someone* free.

I just doubt it'll be me.

## Chapter Nine
# KATARINA

It can't be. It just can't.

Not tonight, of all nights.

I blink fast, gripping my clutch bag tight in my fist.

It must have been a ghost.

And then his face appears again. It's in the distance, amid sweaty bodies moving and shaking to the dance beats, but it's him.

I'd stake my life on it.

But why would he be here? At Max's club on opening night? When he lives on the other side of the country?

Blood rushes between my ears, muting the sounds of electronica and laughter. It's been a long time, but I'd recognize him anywhere.

Strong jaw, deep set black eyes, longish hair that always looks sexed up.

It looks just like Remy.

My breath hitches, and I grab onto the side of the wall for balance. Suddenly, my limbs turn into limp noodles and an ache in my chest reminds me what happened the last time I saw him.

I always wondered what I'd do if I saw him again, if my feelings would be the same as they were years ago.

They're not. In fact, the only feeling that consumes me at this moment is nausea.

So much for young love.

My stomach roils and beads of perspiration form along the back of my neck. I flex my toes and walk around the side of the bar. I have to get out of here. Panic sets in, and I try to calm my breathing.

It can't have been him. How would it even be possible since he lives on the other side of the country? I press my fingertips to my temples, but the throbbing continues.

*This is not real.* I repeat those words to myself over and over. I've been such a wreck lately that I must have made it up in my head. That's the only reasonable explanation.

I cannot lose my shit here. Rocco's rejection, my near-brawl in the ladies' room, and now this?

It was a bad idea to come tonight, and now I'm stuck because there might be more vodka running through my veins than blood.

I fumble in my bag for my phone and pull it out, my hand shaking. I order an Uber, praying it'll be here fast, and within five minutes, I'm sliding into the back of a Toyota Corolla.

It's not until my head leans against that leather cushion that I allow the tears to fall. They fall in silence as I twist my hands together. My condo isn't too far from the club, and I drag myself out of the car after grunting something about having a good night to my driver. They were the only words we'd exchanged, and that was fine with me. Some Uber drivers never shut the hell up, but Aaron didn't say boo once we exchanged hellos.

Thank you, Aaron...

I unlock the door to the building and clutch my stomach. Beaten down is the best description for how I feel, and there's only one person I want here to comfort me.

Even though he's partially to blame for said nausea.

I slowly lean into the door to open it, debating whether or

not to text him. I scoff at the idea in my mind. What in the hell would I even say?

*Hey, Rocco, I know you just rejected me in the most humiliating way possible, but I'm really upset and could use a friend to talk to right now. See, I think I saw my old boyfriend at the club, and I haven't seen him since the day my mother and sister were butchered by some lunatic. And since tomorrow is the anniversary of their death, I'm a little weirded out. Can you come over?*

"Argh!" I throw my fists into the air when a strong hand grips the back of my coat, shoving me inside the lobby.

I don't pause to think; I just twist around and shrug out of my assailant's grip, launching my fist straight into his throat. "Get the fuck off of me!"

Then I gasp and cover my mouth. "Alexi!"

He's doubled over on the ground, clutching his throat, gargling words.

I fall to my knees next to him and throw an arm around his shoulders. "What the hell were you thinking? I could have killed you!"

He holds his neck, narrowing his eyes at me. "You are sick, you know that? Do you ever *not* throw a kill punch?"

"Listen, consider yourself lucky that I've had a lot to drink tonight and my aim was a little off."

He rolls his eyes and pulls himself up to a sitting position against the leather couch in the lobby. "Even drunk you've got pretty damn good aim."

"It's a gift, I guess." I shrug. "What are you doing here?"

"I've been waiting here for you to get back," he rasps, coughing a little bit. "Your father told you how dangerous it is for you to be out by yourself, but you never listen. You always do what you want to do, fuck the consequences."

I force my lips upward. "Well, let's examine the facts, shall we? I could have killed you back there, by myself, and without a weapon. I think I'm pretty good on my own, don't you?"

"I'm one person. These people, these enemies, they travel in packs. They're waiting for you to make one stupid move, and you've been making a lot of them lately."

I let out a deep sigh. "I needed some space. I'm sorry for ignoring you."

"I know it's a hard time for you. Nobody understands that more than me. And your father..." Alexi's eyes grow harder by the second. "He doesn't give a fuck what you're going through. He just holes himself up in some fancy hotel room and drinks the day away, same as he's done every year since it happened. He runs away from it all, leaving you on your own to deal with it."

"Everybody grieves differently."

"He's a fucking coward."

My eyes widen. "This from the man who has worshipped the ground Papa walks on for as many years as I can remember?"

"Yeah, well, let's just say for a long time I didn't see things so clearly."

My brow furrows. "Alexi, did something happen? Why all the hostility? Is it because you really didn't want gym duty?" I try to lighten the mood, even in the depths of my own despair, but his face remains impassive.

He clears his throat a few times and finally shakes his head. "No, nothing happened. I'm just frustrated, that's all. It's not fair to you, the way he handles things and buries things under the rug. You shouldn't have to guess his reasons for acting. You should know the truth."

I put my hand on Alexi's arm. The truth. Yes, I deserve that much. "I shouldn't let you get away with talking like this, you know. He is my father, after all. And he treats you like a son."

Alexi turns his harsh gaze on me. "Yep. And that's what makes it even harder to accept."

I lean my head against his shoulder. "I don't question his decisions," I lie. "I know he has good reasons for making them."

"Too bad for him you're not the only judge and jury out there watching," Alexi grunts, his words like a sharp knife dicing away at my insides. He's telling me something without saying the words, and the chill in his voice clenches my gut.

But his tone drips with disdain. It's hateful...threatening...and dangerous.

I get the message loud and clear.

Even though Papa is not winning any Dad of the Year awards, he's still my father.

And something he taught me a very long time ago always rings clear.

Keep your friends close and your enemies closer.

Words to live by, especially in this life.

You just can't trust anyone.

## Chapter Ten

# ROCCO

"I don't like you."

I nod my head. "That's too bad, Vik, because I really like *you*."

Well, at least it sounded good in my head.

I might get a metal spike to the eye if I try to say them out loud.

I try a different tactic. "I realize I'm an acquired taste."

He rolls his eyes. "You were not my pick for this job, but under the circumstances, it makes sense."

'I'm not following."

"Keeping an eye on Katarina? The job I am asking you to do for me?"

"That's why I'm here?" I lean back in the chair and fold my arms. "I thought it was about the horse farm."

Viktor looks confused. It's a funny mental picture to have. I've never seen him look anything but menacing. This almost makes him seem human.

Snap!

And file!

"Didn't Nico talk to you?"

I let out a chuckle. "Everything with Nico is on a need-to-know basis. And you know how that goes? Nobody needs to know. That's really his bottom line, so to answer your question, no. He didn't tell me anything. I just assumed—"

"We both know how *that* goes." Viktor lifts a dark eyebrow. He looks like shit today. Thinner. Tired. His face is drawn, his eyes heavy and sunken. Still in his signature Armani, but it just hangs lifeless.

Like the rest of him.

"I'm heading out of town for the day, so I appreciate you coming down here so early."

"Just tell me what you need."

He gives me a long, hard look. "Katarina is in danger."

No shit, Sherlock. "I'm aware. What do you want me to do about it?"

"The horse farm was the original plan to keep her safe. To keep both of you safe," he adds.

That was a nice touch. Maybe there's hope for us after all.

"But it seems to have been compromised." Viktor rubs the back of his head. "Our surveillance put an untraceable SUV with bogus plates right in the vicinity. That means the location has been exposed, and it's no longer safe up there."

I swallow a groan. Why in the fuck am I hearing this from Viktor *now*? I just saw Nico last night. Fucking guy couldn't have let me in on the secret? But I can't say that. You never sell out the family. And that goes double for the boss. "I didn't know. Nico didn't mention anything to me." I lean forward, my voice dropping even though the door to Viktor's office at Red Square, his 'social club' is closed and locked tight.

Can't take any chances.

"Viktor, why do you want me to look after Kat? I'm in enough trouble. Why put her in the line of fire?"

He glowers at me and taps his fingertips against the desk. "Because the people who are coming after her are the same ones coming after you and I believe that together, you can take care of each other."

"You really believe that?"

"No, but Nico does. He trusts you. Says you're his top enforcer, a fact which I find hard to believe." He shrugs and lights a skinny black cigarette. He takes a deep pull and blows a thin stream of smoke into the air.

"I'm pretty badass," I say, a smirk playing at my lips.

He says nothing, just stares through narrowed eyes.

Inhales. Exhales. Glares.

I'm slowly choking to death, but still I manage to look unaffected.

Top enforcer. Fuck, yeah. I'll focus on that than being poisoned by secondhand smoke.

"I need to make sure Katarina is kept safe."

"You do know your daughter can probably take on any army of thugs singlehandedly, right? With or without a weapon?"

"I'm well aware of her abilities. I trained her."

"So why do you need me? Why not have your guy Alexi watch her?" I float his name out there, trying somewhat to hide my distaste for that guy. It doesn't really work.

Viktor's expression tenses for a split second, so fast, I almost question whether or not I actually witnessed it. A long pause follows before he opens his mouth to speak. "You know, one of the things I like best about Nico is his ability to sense danger and deceit."

I nod and wait for more exposition, hoping he doesn't talk me in circles again.

"He knows how to avoid it and how to protect the ones he cares about."

"Yes," I agree. He does. He just has a fucked-up way of going about it.

"He surrounds himself with people who carry out his directives, not because he's lining their pockets, but because they believe in him. They have blind faith, if you will."

Fucking A right. Blind faith. That's a good way of putting it. Nico always knows. Nico always protects. Nico always defends.

"He takes care of his own," I say, finally contributing something of value.

Viktor nods. "That's why I asked you to come down here. Let me be clear. I had my doubts about you, still do." His blue eyes narrow to slits yet again as he takes another long drag on the cigarette. "But I don't question his judgment. And while I'm away taking care of my business, I need you to look after my interests here."

Okay, so he basically just told me he doesn't trust his own guys with his daughter. He trusts Nico more than 'his own.'

That's fucked up.

"I'll take care of it. Of *her*." I don't understand why there's so much urgency, but I don't dare ask the question. Always look like you know what the hell you're doing even when you don't. Ignorance is definitely *not* bliss in our line of work.

My fingers are itching to dial Nico's number, to find out why he let me come into the city to meet Viktor, blind as a bat.

"She won't be easy to handle," he says, his voice grave. "You'll need to get to her as soon as possible and keep her close. Just find a way." Viktor pushes his chair back and stands up. "And, Rocco," he says.

"Yeah?"

"Keep this conversation to yourself, along with everything else you know. Katarina must not hear anything about it. Do you understand? If she finds out..." He sighs, his shoulders sagging. "It will be deadly for all of us."

An understatement if I ever heard one.

That much I know for sure.

*Chapter Eleven*

# KATARINA

"**H**appy birthday to us! Happy birthday to us! Happy birthday, happy birthday....happy birthday to us!"

Lili groans when I bounce on her bed with a heaping tray of her favorite breakfast foods. "What time is it?" she says in a groggy voice. Her eyes open a crack and then shut again. "Wait, I don't want to know. Don't answer. I'm going back to sleep."

I put the tray on the nightstand and snuggle up next to my sister. "How can you sleep? It's our sixteenth birthday! We're going to have such an amazing day! And the party tomorrow night?" I let out a squeal. "Oh my God, it's going to be epic!"

Lili flips over and glares at me. "I'd love to be excited at this ungodly hour, and I would be if my darling sister hadn't woken me up at two a.m. when she finally decided to sneak back into the house after slutting it up with her boyfriend."

I giggle and reach out to tickle her underarms. That always gets her. She tries to keep a straight face, but it's impossible. It's her trigger, and I use it whenever I need to wiggle back into her good graces. "Oh, come on, don't be mad! We were just doing a little pre-birthday celebrating, that's all!"

"Yeah, well, I didn't need details. Especially in the middle of the freaking night!"

"You could have pretended to be asleep."

"You could have not stomped around like an elephant when you got home."

"Oh! You did not just call me an elephant!"

I dig my fingers in until she's gasping for air. "Kat! St-stop!" she rasps. "I can't br-breathe!" Now we're both hysterical, and it's already the perfect start to our special day.

"Listen, I made you all of your favorite foods! I'm trying to make it up to you, okay? Don't be mad at me," I say in a sing-song voice, wiggling my fingers at her. "You know what I'll do if you don't forgive me! Say it! Come on!"

Lili shoves herself away from me and lets out a yelp as she tumbles onto the carpet. "Stay away from me with those evil fingers!"

I let out a wicked chuckle and inch closer to her. "You'd better say it or else!"

She chuckles and rolls even farther away, grabbing her robe. "Fine! I give! You win!"

"Say it! Say I'm forgiven and that I'm the best sister you could have ever asked for!"

"Yeah, yeah, yeah." Lili rounds the bed and makes a grab for the tray. "You're forgiven."

"And?"

"You're the best, okay?" She rolls her eyes and grabs a slice of whole wheat toast. It's the only kind of bread we have, so I made sure to slather it in butter and strawberry jelly. She loves it that way but never gives in to the temptation. She's so disciplined. But today, she needs to live a little. I'm thinking pizza for dinner, too...

Me? I eat whatever the hell I want when I want it. If my gymnastics leotard busts open, I'll just get a new one.

"Mmm," she mumbles, shoving the rest of the slice into her mouth. "God, that's good."

I beam. "I knew you'd love it!"

She chews for a minute, eyeing me in a way that tells me she has something on her mind other than my fabulous birthday breakfast buffet. "What's it like to be in love?"

My eyes pop open wide. "Oh, um..." I tilt my head to the side, thinking about my answer. "Well, it's a little hard to explain. I never really thought about how to describe it before."

"Try," she says, her blue eyes focused on my face. "I really want to know."

"I'm sure it's different for everyone, but..." I think for a second and my lips instinctively curl upward. "It's impossible not to smile when I think of Remy. When he's around me, there's a fluttery feeling right here that never goes away." I rub a hand over my belly and take a deep breath. "Everything tingles when he kisses me. And when he's gone, I feel cold all over, like something is missing. And when he's back, I'm warm again. Cozy. Happy." I shrug. "Does that sound really stupid?"

"No," Lili whispers, a faraway smile on her face. "It's really sweet. So unlike you." She makes a face and ducks just before the throw pillow I hurl at her makes contact with her head. "I'd like to find a guy who makes me feel like that. Maybe someday."

But that someday never came. That conversation was the last one we'd had about love...the last we'd ever have.

I haven't felt those things since.

And I don't know if I ever will because it would mean I'd have to give someone a fighting chance to *make* me feel them.

I pull open the door to the animal shelter, a heavy weight sitting in my gut. A knot of tears sits in the back of my throat, but I won't let them out. I can't.

Again, I've managed to avoid Alexi, but sooner or later, he'll come looking for me. He'll try the gym first. That's where I would usually go.

But today, I need a different environment...one where I won't feel so alone, where I can cry and nobody will judge or ask questions or speak at all, for that matter. It's one where I can get a hug without having to worry about tomorrow or the next day. No strings, no conditions, no risk of having my throat slit.

It'll just be me and my animals.

The door closes behind me, and I flip on the lights. I knew nobody would be here today. The person who runs the shelter takes the weekends off, leaving me alone to tend to the animals. I barely see her. We cross paths here and there, and she leaves me lots of sticky notes, but for the most part, I work alone.

Exactly the way I like it.

I pad across the floor, my flip-flops flapping as I walk down the hallway to greet my friends. I'd never be caught dead in flip-flops any other day, but this self-imposed solitude makes me happy to dress in sweats. My hair is thrown into a messy ponytail, and the only makeup I'm wearing is concealer to hide the dark circles under my eyes.

I'm always a mess on the inside.

Today, the outside matches.

"Morning, babies," I murmur, reaching down to pet one of the mutts who barks in appreciation. "Are you hungry?"

I give them all a little stroke as I head toward the supply room. I pull out large bags of food and start the rounds. The noise dials up from zero to a hundred when I appear with breakfast, and it's a welcome change from the sounds of my past, the ones that perpetually haunt my mind and torment my ears. I open the cages, giving the animals a chance to stretch their legs a little as I pour the food into their bowls. The owner has warned me about this, but it doesn't stop me. They need a taste of freedom every once in a while.

I kneel down in front of Stoli 2's cage, running a hand down the front of it. The tears sting my eyes, and the sob erupts from my throat. I don't bother to hold it back any longer.

The tears spill over, streaming down my un-made-up face. I don't bother to wipe them away. They drip onto my clothes and the floor, my sorrow pooling around my feet. Some of the animals wander over, sensing my distress. They creep closer, nesting their heads in my side, in my chest, and against my back.

My body quakes against their furry ones, and I reach down to hug them tight. They don't pull away, they don't ask questions. They just let me grieve.

I don't know how long I sit there. Time passes, but it's inconsequential. It could be minutes or hours.

It doesn't change anything.

Life hasn't gotten easier or more bearable.

Yeah, I put up a strong front, but it's bullshit. I'm always a second away from shattering like an empty bottle of vodka hitting a concrete wall.

I'm still alone.

I'm still suffering.

And I'm still a goddamn wreck.

The sobs finally quiet, and I sit back against the wall, letting out a deep sigh. All of the stress and tension drain from my body. I'm spent — physically, emotionally, mentally. I only allow this catharsis once a year, and it takes me that long to recover and prepare for the next one.

I drag myself to my feet and usher the animals back into their cages so they can eat. I needed that today, more than I needed to pound the shit out of a heavy bag.

Or Alexi.

*Ding!*

Speaking of...

I lock up the cages so the animals don't go running for the door. I grit my teeth and jog toward the front of the shelter when I hear the call bell. How the hell did someone get inside? Didn't I lock the door?

Um, no. I clearly forgot since there's someone inside! Dammit, I really need to get my head screwed on straight.

I tuck a stray strand of hair behind my ear, huffing a bit as I approach the front of the shelter. It must be Alexi. I sent him home last night after I was safely inside my condo. I promised I'd call him as soon as I woke up, but after everything he *didn't* say last night, he was the last person I wanted to talk to this morning. He's been texting me for the past couple of hours, and I haven't responded. He must know by now that I'm not at the gym. This is the only other place I'd be, other than my favorite bar.

And I'm heading there next.

My cell phone vibrates, and I pull it out of the waistband of my sweatpants.

*Where the fuck are you? If I tell your father that you ran off again by yourself, he'll kill both of us!*

*Ding!*

Okay, so it's not Alexi ringing the bell. Great. It's some random person who obviously can't read and insists on ringing that damn bell. I mean, the sign says Closed, for Christ's sake! I roll my eyes. "Coming!" I already hate this person, who the fuck ever it is. I wipe under my eyes one more time, praying that the evidence of my earlier hysterics have magically vanished.

I round the corner and plaster on a smile for the guy with his back to me, hoping I don't look like too much of a train wreck. "Hi, can I help you?"

He slowly turns, and I choke back a gasp, my hands flying up to my messy ponytail. "Jesus Christ! What the hell are you doing here?"

Rocco steps toward me, and I instinctively back away. "Kat..." he says, his eyebrows furrowed.

"Yes, it's me!" I throw my hands into the air. "Okay? This is how I really look! I'm shorter than you, I don't roll out of bed wearing ten pounds of makeup, and I do own sweats!" I shove past him and lock the front door so I don't have any more unwelcome visitors, today of all days, when I just want to be alone.

I flip the lock and turn around, my arms folded over my chest. "Now tell me why you're here."

He grins. "You look different, but fuck, that fire still rages, huh?"

I roll my eyes and shove him away as I walk back down the hall toward the animals. "Why don't you just fuck off? I don't know why you're here anyway. You made it pretty clear last night that you're not interested in anything with me." I bite my lower lip. Shit, that came out sounding a little scorned.

"That's why I came." His sneakers pound on the tiled floor behind me as he runs to catch up. "Something was up with you last night."

"Something was up with you, too." I toss him a quick, sidelong glance and cock an eyebrow. "But I'm guessing it didn't stay that way for long. Or did you go back to find your whorey groupies after you blew me off?"

"Would you just stop for a minute?" He grabs my wrist and gently tugs it. I don't pull away, I just stare down at his fingers. They're not loosening at all, even when I give him my best death glare.

"You made it pretty clear that you're not into...whatever this is." I shrug. "It could have been fun, but it's fine. *I'm* fine, if that's what you were worried about."

He narrows his eyes at me. "You don't look fine."

I twist out of his vise-like grip and poke him in the chest. "If you think this is because of you..." I let out a dry laugh and shake my head. "You're insane."

"Then tell me, Kat. Tell me what's going on. I mean, you're usually a bitch on wheels, but there's something else happening here. I've never seen you like that, okay? I just want to know—"

I clutch the sides of my head. "Stop! Just stop! If there was anything I wanted to talk to you about, I would sooner kill myself for giving a shit, okay?"

"You don't need to do this. You think you have to act so tough all the time to hide what you're really feeling, but it's—"

"Fuck you! Don't pretend that you know me at all!" I grab the sides of his jacket and push him against the wall. I stare up at him because the damn flip-flops subtract about five inches from my height. But size has nothing on my anger. "Fucking you would have been fun. Period. Maybe I just needed that last night. I sure as hell don't need it now, so if you're back here for another shot, think again. Offer's off the table."

"I didn't come here for sex."

"Then why did you come, Rocco?" I yell. "I don't need a therapist! I am just fine!" Tears sting my eyes and spill over, rushing down the sides of my face like the world is ending. Oh yeah, mine already did. "Just fucking fine!"

The expression on his face is priceless. If I wasn't so tormented by grief right now, I think I might actually laugh. He has no idea how to react right now, no clue what to do or say. I never thought I'd see the day that Rocco Lucchese would be silenced by a woman, especially a crazed woman who is losing her goddamned mind. "Kat," he whispers.

"Leave! Just fucking leave!" I pound on his chest with my fists. "Get the hell out of here! I don't need you! I don't need anyone!" My shoulders quake, my breaths short and sharp. I swipe at the tears blurring my vision but they don't stop. Just when I thought I'd cried for ten lifetimes, they start again.

Will they ever stop?

"I'm not leaving."

"I hate you!" I scream, launching my fist at his face. He doesn't even try to block it, even though my wind-up is hella sloppy. He could have grabbed my wrist, could have stopped it from connecting with his jaw.

He didn't.

He let it happen.

He took the shot.

I want to throw myself into his arms right now. I want to feel them wrapped around me. I want him to kiss me again...oh, shit.

What the hell is going on?

Hot mess doesn't even begin to describe me right now.

A thin trickle of blood drizzles from the side of his mouth and he wipes it away with his sleeve. I should give him a tissue. Or some ice. Or an apology.

Instead, I just stand there, glowering at him.

"You're a real piece of work, you know that?"

I purse my lips. "You're a real asshole for—"

"For what? Caring? Wanting to make sure you're okay?" he yells.

"Who asked you?" I screech. "I never asked you to care! I can't believe you're Nico's top enforcer! Is this how you deal with the enemy? You talk them to death? Get them to open up and listen to their gripes about the family? Show them how sensitive you are to their issues?"

"Wait, he said I'm his top enforcer?"

I stop pacing and look at him, my eyes wide. "*That's* your takeaway?"

He shrugs with a lopsided grin on his face. "It's a big compliment. He could've said it was Max. But let's be real, Max is a loose cannon. I'm just more level-headed. He likes that."

My jaw drops, nearly hitting the floor. "Are we really having this conversation right now?"

"Seems so." He places his hands on my shoulders and leans his head down so that his lips are so close to mine...close enough that I can smell spearmint on his breath, and oh God, I want to taste...

Argh! No! I lost control once. I don't plan to make it a habit. I swing my arms up and around, knocking his hands off of me. "I asked you to leave."

"You didn't ask anything, Kat. Maybe if you had, I would have listened. Instead, you clocked me in the jaw!"

"Because you weren't listening to me."

"Wasn't I?" His eyes narrow. "I was listening. That's why I'm here right now. I heard everything you said last night. I heard everything you shouted at me just now."

"Then that should have been enough," I whisper, my fists tight against my sides.

"It's not. I know you need something."

"You don't know shit," I hiss.

"I know you attacked those girls in the club last night, but you didn't tear them to shreds."

"I didn't feel like breaking a nail." I don't bother to ask how he found out about my little altercation. People who live our lives have eyes and ears everywhere.

And truth be told, I wanted him to find out.

I wanted him to confront me about it.

I wanted to see if someone actually gave a damn about me.

"Bullshit. You walked away for a reason."

"Maybe because I didn't think you were worth it." I turn away from him, trying to slow my racing pulse. But damn, it throbs hard against my neck, and I don't know if it's anger or desire that's making the blood bubble in my veins.

"Was it really about me? Or was it more about you?"

"Maybe I just felt sorry for her. Her nose job was botched enough. I didn't want to make it any worse."

He snickers. "You're un-fucking-believable."

I don't want to smile, but my lips betray me. They curl upward. I bite back the giggle in the back of my throat, but it manages to escape anyway.

"I was hoping I'd eventually see that human side of you again." He winks. "I thought that I imagined it."

"You shouldn't have come here," I say, my smile fading. "I want to be alone."

"Then you should have remembered to lock the front door." He steps closer to me, his voice low and husky. "But I would have gotten to you eventually."

Lust swirls around my head, fogging up my mind and clouding my sensibilities. The electricity between us crackles, and the heat in his gaze ignites the flickering embers in my belly. They shoot out to every limb, scorching every cell, and he hasn't even laid a finger on me.

I feel drunk. Disoriented. Unsteady.

And for the first time in a long time, I'm not numb.

That scares me more than anything else.

I back away from Rocco, my hands flying up to my temples. No, no, no! This isn't happening. This is just physical, nothing more.

*It can't be more. I have nothing to offer him...or anyone, for that matter.*

*I just want to be alone!*

*Or...do I?*

*Say something...say something! Anything! Just keep your distance. Letting him in is too dangerous.*

"How's um...Stoli 2?" It's the only thing I can come up with, and even croaking out his name forms a thick knot of tears in my throat. The memories...goddammit...they come rushing back like a tidal wave, crashing over me and whipping me left, right, upside down, and inside out.

And before he even has a chance to respond, my hands fly up to my mouth in an attempt to prevent the hysterics from wracking my body yet again.

Too late...

But this time, I let it happen. I don't try to hold back.

Because I really don't want to be alone. I want someone to hold me, to tell me it will be okay, that it really wasn't my fault, that I'm not to blame for everything. I need to hear that, need to believe it, if I have any hope of ever recovering from that day.

So when he pulls me into his arms, I allow myself to fall into them, breathing in the scent of his cologne until it makes me dizzy. The tears flow from my eyes and his arms tighten around me in response. It only makes me cry harder.

Time pretty much stops, and I don't care if I stay here wrapped in his embrace forever. He holds me, rubbing a hand down my back as my sobs finally quiet. Even after I told him... actually, screamed at him...that I hate him.

*Is he a glutton for punishment or what?*

He doesn't speak at all, and thank fuck for that because I have no idea what is happening to me and I'm afraid of what may come spewing out of my mouth if I open it. His fingers stroke the back of my neck and my spine suddenly morphs into a limp spaghetti noodle. Ohhh...what is he doing with those magical fingers? He's making me forget, distracting me from the toxins flooding my veins, all by innocently targeting an erogenous zone I never even knew existed.

My knees buckle, my arms tentatively reaching around his muscular back.

I'm not a hugger. At least, I'm not anymore.

But this...I could get used to this.

His head drops on top of mine, his warm lips resting against my hair. Goosebumps shoot up my arms and down my legs, despite the fact that they're covered in velour. I've never been so affected by...sentiment.

Holy crap.

Who the hell am I?

A shiver slithers across my skin in the wake of his fingertips. "Mmm," I moan.

"So that's what you like, huh?"

"Stop talking."

"So I'm just supposed to stand here all day and listen to you moan like that?"

"Yes."

"Do you like torturing me?"

"I hope that's a rhetorical question. I like torturing most people."

"It doesn't seem like you want to rip out my throat right now."

"I told you to stop talking."

"I like your shampoo. It smells good."

I pull my head away from his chest and stare up at him. "I tell you to stop talking and you tell me my shampoo smells good?"

He shrugs, that adorable half-smirk teasing his lips. "It does. I figured you might like to know that."

"I don't care about my shampoo."

"It smells like something sweet...some fruity shit." His grin widens. "You don't seem like the sweet and fruity type."

"They don't scent shampoo with vodka." That sexy smirk.

Dammit, it's contagious.

He tightens his grip on me. "See, you complained about the talking thing, but at least it got you smiling. That makes me feel like I'm safe, and that you're not gonna pull a knife on me or something for getting too close." A shadow crosses his face. "I wouldn't have adopted Stoli 2 if I knew you'd miss him this much."

"No, you did a good thing for him. He needed a home, and me trying to keep him here wouldn't have been fair to him."

"Do you want to see him today? It looks like you can use a friend right now, and if it's not gonna be me, it may as well be Stoli 2."

I sniffle and push away from him. I need distance, but the urge to crawl back into him is so strong, it has me faltering. "I didn't want to fall apart like this...in front of you...in front of anyone..." I tighten my ponytail and move around the desk so there is at least some physical barrier between us since my emotional fortress crumbled like a stale cookie under the pads of his fingertips. "It was never supposed to happen."

"We all have bad days."

"I've had more than my fair share."

"So come home with me." He sweeps a hand through his hair. "I promise I won't try to take advantage of you. I don't have a death wish or anything."

I bite down on my lower lip. Seeing Stoli 2 and holding his furry body tight...I need that, a reminder of something good in my life. I feel closer to Lili and Mom through him. I know it sounds ridiculous, but his presence always brought me comfort, something I desperately crave right now.

"Okay," I whisper, twisting my ponytail around my fingers. "Just for a little while."

His lips curl upward, and my breath hitches. From a freaking smile.

I really need to dial back this vulnerability bullshit. It's not a good look for me.

## Chapter Twelve
## ROCCO

I watch as Kat pulls out a rubber band and fluffs out her hair. It spills down her back in long waves, and I really hope she leaves it loose. My fingers twitch, the sensation of fisting those soft dark strands still vivid in my memory.

*That's not why you're here...*

I don't know what I expected by coming over here today after that scene in the club. The Closed sign told the world she didn't want company.

But I had a job to do, and I found her, like I said I would.

I just had no idea she was having a nervous breakdown.

Something happened, something she's not telling me. It's why she came after me last night and attacked me on the dance floor. I'd like to believe it was because she feels the same way about me that I do about her, but I'm not an idiot.

Kat doesn't do feelings.

She does guns. And knives. And ice picks.

And I think today probably shocked her as much as it did me.

Still, she agreed to come home with me.

Maybe I can get her to talk after all.

Anything to keep her close.

Safe.

Wine would loosen her up. Screw the vodka. Her body is immune to the shit by now.

She runs her fingers through her hair and turns toward me with her bag in hand. There are bright pink spots on her cheeks and her eyes have a little more light in them than they did a while ago.

I help her pack everything away…supplies, food, everything cluttering up the place…and after playing with the animals for a little longer, she's ready to go. I don't push. Kat's a control freak, whether or not she knows it. Better to let her call the shots if I have any chance of getting through to her and hanging on to her until further notice.

"You're a pretty good helper," she murmurs, locking the front door behind her once we're outside. "Thanks for staying with me."

It feels like everything I thought I knew about this woman has changed in the past twenty-four hours.

I mean, I figured I'd come here, find her, and spend the rest of the time ducking while she threw heavy and coma-inducing shit at me for rejecting her last night.

Instead, I found someone very different, someone I didn't know before, and someone I want to get to know a lot better.

She walks toward her car and my mouth finally decides to start working. "Why don't you ride with me?" Part of me says it out of obligation to Viktor, but the other part just wants her next to me.

Under me.

On top of me.

Shit. Here we go.

Repeat after me…

There will be no wine. There will be no sex.

Fuck my life, why can't I stop thinking about her naked for one second?

She furrows her brow. "And leave my car here all night?"

"Well, I can take you back for it tomorrow."

"It's a long drive back here," she says, a smile teasing her lips.

I shrug. "I don't mind. I'm not working until late, anyway."

She pauses for a minute. Longest damn minute I've ever experienced. "Are you going to take me home when I want to leave?"

I swallow hard, past the lump in my throat. Jesus Christ, what the hell is wrong with me? Did I really think we were gonna play sleepover? My insides are twisted like a pretzel right now because of this woman...because I need to be around her, and I'll agree to just about anything right now. "Yeah, whenever you want," I lie. I'll figure out a way to hide her in my bed...er, my house.

She nods and drops her keys into her handbag. "Okay. Lead the way."

I blink fast. "Uh, yeah. Right over here." I lead her to the spot where I parked my car. I open the passenger side door for her and watch her slide into the seat before I jog around the front of the car. "Goddammit!" I pull out the parking ticket from my windshield and groan as I sink into the driver's seat. I shove the ticket into the center console.

"You didn't read the sign?"

I roll my eyes and press the ignition button to start the car. "I did, but I figured I'd be in and out of here before my time was up."

"Why?" She turns a curious glance my way, and I snicker, maneuvering the car onto the road.

"I kinda figured you'd have sent me packing after kicking my ass for last night."

"Oh." She giggles. "Yeah, I was a little distracted, I guess."

"Rain check?"

"Definitely."

We laugh for a minute before the silence consumes us both, leaving me to my thoughts. Again.

Christ, maybe I'm the one who needs the wine.

I don't know why I even bothered to look for her today. This thing between us isn't the forever kind.

Time is running out.

At least for me it is.

"Rocco."

"Yeah?" Even hearing her say my name makes my cock twitch. It's like being sixteen all over again.

"I'm glad you came looking for me today."

"Me, too."

"You ever wonder how things might be different for you if your family never knew the Salesis?"

I press my foot on the brake and slow at a red light. "Sometimes. But it's not like it keeps me up all night or anything. I mean, it is what it is. I just worry about my sister Lindy. We keep her pretty much in the dark about a lot of shit that goes down, but it's not so much my dad anymore. He got hurt years ago. Really fucked up his leg in a car accident. So now he works pretty close to Nico's dad, but he's out of the day-to-day stuff. Plus, he's kinda on the old side." I snicker. "Not really in good enough shape to go toe to toe with the schmucks we deal with, you know?"

Kat nods, staring out the window. Is she wishing for a different life, one where her mom and sister are still alive? One where she doesn't have to slit throats or pop caps or bash in skulls? One where she can just be normal?

What the fuck is normal, anyway?

"I don't ever wonder," she whispers. "I already know the answer."

I can't say anything. I'm not supposed to know about her past, why she's here in Jersey, and why her father has turned her into a lethal assassin.

And most of all, I'm not supposed to know who killed her family.

But I know all of it, things she doesn't even know.

And if I don't want to end up like her mom and sister, I need to keep my damn mouth shut even though I can feel her pain. Her body is tense and stiff, her voice sad. She needs closure, but it'll get her killed.

That must be why Viktor wants to keep her in the dark. He knows as well as I do what she'll do with that information.

So I keep driving, listening to her deep and even breaths.

The silence in the car is deafening. It forces me to think about things...things I don't want looping through my mind. Nico, the horse farm, the Cinques, Viktor. All things that represent my fate in some way, shape, or form. And based on recent events, my fate ain't too pretty.

I flip through the scenarios in my mind, absently wondering why Lindy hasn't texted me so far today. She was supposed to let me know what time she'd be over with Stoli 2, and judging by Kat's emotional state, I really don't think she can handle my family today of all days.

Traffic is kind of light right now, and soon enough, we'll be at my place. If I don't have Stoli 2, she's gonna think I lured her there under false pretenses.

My place. God, I'd wanted to get Kat to my house and on her back more times than I can count.

False pretenses. Huh. Not exactly.

I peek out of the corner of my eye a few minutes later to find Kat's head bobbing to the side. Her eyes are closed, and her mouth is hanging open. Not much, but enough to make me smirk.

It must mean she's relaxed, right? Comfortable? Content?

That, or she's just exhausted emotionally, and passed out from the stress and pressure.

I flip on my turn signal and nod. That must be it.

My iPhone buzzes in my pocket, and I pull it out, peering at the screen as I tap my foot on the brake at a red light in my neighborhood. It's Lindy.

*Just got back from a walk with Stoli 2. He's eating right now. Come over and pick him up?*

I let out a low groan. I really didn't want a pit stop.

"What's wrong?" Kat murmurs, twisting her body toward me. Her eyes are hooded and heavy with sleep.

"Stoli 2 is at my parents' house. Lindy had him last night and just got back from walking him. I've, ah, got to pick him up." I look over at her, not sure what to expect. Maybe she'll volunteer to stay in the car. I can't see that she'd be open to meeting my family—

She shrugs and a lazy smile lifts her lips. "Okay. Do I look presentable enough to meet everyone?"

My mouth drops open. "Are you serious?"

She sits up straight, her eyes wide. "Oh my God, do I look that horrible?"

*Honk! Honk!*

I let out a string of curses and ease my foot off the brake, maneuvering the car over to the side of the road so the asshole behind me can go. I put the car into Park and turn toward her. "Are you insane, Kat?"

She furrows her brow. "Sometimes...yeah."

I shake my head and tilt her chin up. "You're fucking gorgeous. Always. I just didn't know if you'd be up to being around people, that's all."

A slow smile brightens her face, erasing the shadows and the darkness. It may only be temporary, but fuck me, it's a beautiful sight.

"I'm not exactly the kind of girl you bring home to meet Mom and Dad."

My jaw drops. "That's not what...I mean, I just need to pick up Sto...I'm really not trying..." I rake a hand through my hair and let out a sigh. "Look, what I'm trying to say is that there's no ulterior motive here. I swear. It's all innocent."

Kat lets out a loud chuckle. It's a nice sound, a welcome one...so different from her usual icy and sarcastic tone, I almost forget who I'm sitting next to.

It makes me even more crazy about her, if that's possible.

And truth be told, I want to take her home with me. I want her by my side, even if she doesn't know that. I have to protect her and keeping her with me is the best way to do it. Her enemies are my enemies, and I need to keep her safe. Alexi sure as hell can't keep her in check, and Viktor warned me in not so many words that she'd try to evade him anyway.

She doesn't follow the rules.

It's just her nature.

It's also why we're in this situation.

They call Max a loose cannon, but dammit, Kat is just as bad. She's got the same killer instinct, same impulsive nature. They're a lot alike, which is probably why they get along so well.

Like Kat, Max goes against orders when he thinks it's for the right reason. He doesn't ever worry about consequences or backlash. Also, he loves the kill...can't forget about that.

No wonder why Nico picked me to take on this role instead of Max.

My moral compass doesn't always point due north, but at least I have enough sense to stand down when the shit storm approaches.

And it's coming. Fast and fierce.

"Are you trying to figure out how to explain me to your family?" She narrows her eyes. "Why the hell aren't you driving? Do you want me to change my mind?"

There's an edge to her voice, a hardness that shields all of the other shit she's trying to keep protected. And suddenly, she's back to being the badass I love to hate. Hate to love. Whatever the hell. It's *her*.

"No, I don't want you to change your mind. I want to take you home with me." Shiiiiit. Did I really just say that? "I mean, um, I don't think you should be alone, and it'll, ah, be good for you to eat something..." I clear my throat, a hot flush creeping up the sides of my face. "Not me, of course, I meant like, dinner. And maybe you could use a drink. Or five."

"I'd love to feed you a few drinks and see how *that* goes.

Although I don't know if I could possibly be more entertained than I am at this second," she drawls, a sexy grin lifting her lips.

My body is so overheated, I might just spontaneously combust right here in the front seat. What the fuck am I thinking? And why can't I keep my damn mouth shut? My foot belongs on the brake, not in my throat! "Sorry, um, I didn't mean for things to come out that way. I just...I don't know. You look like you could use a friend."

She nods. "You're right. But I guess you'll have to do."

I let out a snort of laughter. "You're a real charmer, anyone ever tell you that?"

"Yeah, usually when I have them in a chokehold. That's when I hear all the good shit."

I grin at her. "I'd love to be a fly on the wall."

"Well, seeing as how you've been in one of those chokeholds..." She waggles her eyebrows at me. "You have firsthand knowledge about how it all goes down."

I put the car into Drive and press my foot on the gas to merge back into traffic. "Point taken. I'm sure you've heard it all."

Kat lets out a little sigh and leans back against the seat. We sit in silence over the next few minutes until we arrive at my parents' house. They took my recommendation about an impromptu trip down to Boca to visit my grandmother and aunt tomorrow, and I'm sure they're in full-blown packing mode right now. My mom hates when I bring over unannounced guests, especially when the house isn't in perfect order. But there wasn't time to call, and I really need Stoli 2.

*Kat* really needs Stoli 2.

I turn off the engine and get out of the car, jogging around to the other side. I pull open Kat's door and hold out my hand. She grasps it in hers...it's so soft and warm and I don't want to let it go when she's standing in front of me, the perfect height for me to just dip my head and graze my lips with hers...

Until...Lindy.

"Hey! I don't know you were bringing company!" Lindy's excited voice carries over to us at the curb, and I swallow a groan. She's not here so I can make a move on her. She's here to get away from whatever demons are chasing her today. "Mom's going to flip out. The place is a mess because we're still packing!"

"Don't judge," I whisper to Kat. "My mom is gonna be pissed that I'm bringing you here without giving her advance notice of like a month." I shake my head. "Italian moms, what can I say? Their main goal in life is making sure their family is fed well. At least, that's how it is here. Food is king."

Kat giggles. "I'm awesome at ordering takeout."

I clutch my chest in mock horror. "Takeout? That's blasphemy right there. Keep that on lockdown, okay?

She nods, still holding my hand. The streetlights have just flickered on, casting a glow on her face. Her eyes twinkle a bit, and she is finally looking more like herself. The sex kitten-slash-assassin I've come to know, lust after, and fear, if I'm being honest.

She squeezes my hand before dropping it and it hits me like a shot to the chest. I watch her walk past me toward the front door, her hips swaying back and forth in that soft, velvety material. I don't know what it's called, but it's fucking nice, and I'd like to see her wear more of it so I can rub myself all up on her—

Christ, enough! I clutch the sides of my head and follow her up the short staircase. Lindy watches from the family room window and flings open the door to welcome us inside. "Come in! It's freezing! How are you in flip-flops?"

"My feet never get cold." Kat flips her hair over her shoulder and gives me a quick wink before greeting Lindy. "So, I hear you've been taking great care of Stoli 2 for your brother."

At the mention of his name, Stoli 2 comes running from the back of the house, his tongue hanging out of his mouth. He leaps at Kat, barking loudly. He licks her up and down before she can even make it past the foyer. She drops to her feet, wraps her arms around his neck, and he cuddles into her. She grips him so tight, breathing him in like she's trying to capture the memory of everything he represents. Or represented.

Her shoulders shake a bit as she strokes his soft back, and my stomach twists. Is she...crying?

Lindy smiles so wide and hard, I think her face might crack from the pressure. "He's such an amazing dog. I'm so happy Rocco adopted him. And," She continues, her smile getting wider if that's even possible. "I'm so happy that you've come to help babysit him! You know, Stoli 2, not my brother." Lindy chuckles at her own joke. "Not that Rocco couldn't use a babysitter. Especially with his job as the bouncer at Nico's dance club. He's just asking for trouble every time he goes to work!"

Kat lifts an eyebrow at me, and I give her a little shrug. Little white lies. They serve to protect. Lindy doesn't need to know what I actually do for a living. I don't need her worrying about the shit I deal with on a daily basis. Better that she thinks I just judge half-naked chicks and pick and choose which ones I want to let inside the club. It's better than the bullshit I fed her about why I'd been out in California in the first place. Trying to make it as an actor when the closest I'd come to performing was beating the shit out of the drama teacher when he got a little too handsy with Max's sister Shaye.

Maybe Lindy believed it, maybe she didn't.

But she never questioned it.

Sometimes I think we all want to live in our own little bubbles where things are safe and happy and free from bullets and baseball bats.

Lindy looks from me to Kat and back to me before tearing into the kitchen. "Mom! Dad! Rocco is here! With a friend!" The glee is dripping from her lips, and it's hard for me not to laugh. "Sorry," I mouth to Kat.

She shrugs and walks into the kitchen with Stoli 2 on her heels, ready to face whatever is waiting.

"Oh, my goodness!" My mother exclaims, and I can just hear

the panic in her tone. "I'm so sorry for the mess! We weren't expecting company, but I'm so glad to meet you...?"

"Kat." Kat holds out a hand and grasps my mother's uncertain one.

"Her real name is Katarina," Lindy hisses, nudging my mother. "Isn't that so glamorous?"

Mom nods, her eyes lighting up like the fireplace in our living room, where she's packing five huge suitcases. Clothes and shoes litter the floor and couch, and there's an assortment of hats and tubes of suntan lotion spread out on the coffee table. "Kat, it is such a pleasure to meet you. I'm Allegra." Her cheeks turn pink and she motions to the mess in the living room. "I'm so sorry for the disarray. I didn't expect anyone, and we're leaving for Florida tomorrow morning, and I—"

"Please don't apologize," Kat says in a smooth voice. "It's absolutely fine. We shouldn't have intruded like this."

"No, no!" Mom waves her hands in the air. "Nonsense! You're here and Rocco never brings home any, um, friends." Her smile matches Lindy's, and she takes Kat by the arm and leads her to a chair at the large kitchen table. "Please have a seat. I'll make dinner. And how about a glass of wine? Do you like red?"

Kat smiles at my mom's enthusiasm. "I'd love some. Red is my favorite."

Mom claps her hands and hurries over to the wine cabinet, pulling out a bottle of chianti. "This one is fantastic!" She hands it to me. "Would you mind? Dad is upstairs pulling out the rest of his clothes." She smiles at me, but I don't miss the death look in her gaze. I know she's pissed off at me right now, that the first impression Kat will have of my house and my family is a hot mess. And my next words will aggravate her even more, but she's gonna deal. "Ma, don't cook anything. I'll order pizza. You guys are leaving tomorrow. Just sit down and relax for a little while. I didn't mean to throw you off, and I promise we'll be out of your hair soon enough."

My mother gasps and claps a hand over her mouth. "I can't

believe you just said that," she whispers. "My only son. Are you trying to kill me?"

"Ma," I let out an exasperated sigh. "I'm just saying you guys have things to do for tomorrow. I don't want to get in your way, that's all."

"You're never in my way, pumpkin." She wraps her arms around me and squeezes, holding me close so she can whisper in my ear. "She's gorgeous and sweet. Don't screw this up."

I hug my mother tight. "I love you, but you're crazy. And totally off-base," I whisper back. I pull away. "Okay, what kind of pizza does everyone want?"

## Chapter Thirteen
# KATARINA

I watch Rocco embrace his mother, and it brings a smile to my lips to see this otherwise lethal enforcer snicker like a little boy, like he has nothing to fear and everything to live for. He's happy. Genuinely happy. I listen to the quick banter between mother and son—they know each other so well, pushing buttons in a playful way, teasing each other, and just having a good time being with one another.

I used to have that. And for the past eight years, I've missed out on learning more about my mother and sharing my secrets with her. She didn't get to see me grow up, she doesn't know I'm a hollow shell of my former self because of all I've lost. She wasn't there to stop me from making mistakes, she didn't get to see me graduate high school or comfort me when I cried myself to sleep every night. She couldn't fill the void when my dad pulled away, she wasn't there to soothe the ache as I wept for someone to actually notice me and to love me.

She doesn't know I can't even look at chocolate cake without losing it completely because hers was the best in the world, the one she baked for me every year for my birthday and every other time I'd beg, the one that was left out to cool on the stove *that* day.

"Kat, do you like olives?"

I blink fast in an attempt to clear the memories from my vision. "Oh, sure. That's fine."

Rocco winks at me. "Or we could get penne a la vodka pizza. That's right up your alley, you know, without the penne."

I roll my eyes. "Olives are just fine. I'm not picky when it comes to pizza."

"Did someone say pizza?" A booming voice comes from the front hallway and Antonio Lucchese, Rocco's dad, appears in the kitchen a second later, a big smile on his face. I know of him, of course, but I've never actually met him. His grin lights up the room when he sees his son. "You didn't say you were stopping by. I thought we wouldn't get to see you until tomorrow when you drive us to the airport."

Rocco gives his dad a hug and claps him on the back. "I figured you might need dinner after all of the packing you guys have been doing. Take a load off for a while. I just called it in. I didn't want Ma to go crazy making anything when you're leaving tomorrow."

"She let you order *takeout?*" Antonio's incredulous voice makes me giggle, like it's truly a mortal sin to dial ten little numbers and ask for someone else to cook your food. He turns his head toward me, eyes widening. "Well, well. Who do we have here?"

"Dad, this is Katarina Ivanov."

I watch the realization sink in, and his lips stretch into a warm smile. He crosses the kitchen, and I get up to shake his hand. "It's nice to finally meet you."

He gently bats away my hand and gives me a big hug. "This is what we do in our house."

I breathe in and a smile teases my lips. He smells so good, so clean and just...well, safe. With his kind face and round belly, how could I feel anything but? This man was the right hand of Nico's dad for years before he retired and handed the family over to Nico. I'd heard a lot about him from Nico when I first showed up on the scene. But I also knew he'd been injured pretty badly, so he's taken a backseat in the family operations since then. He still advises Nico and does work with some of the other families, business planning, things like that. Anything that keeps him off his feet.

He's been on the sidelines for years now, and only recently got involved when the family was battling with the Cappodamos, a rival family from New York. Things escalated pretty quickly, and that's when Nico tagged me in.

Good thing, too, since he, Max, and Rocco were like the Three Blind Mice without me.

Sometimes, plans just need a woman's touch.

"I've heard a lot about you from Rocco and Nico," Antonio says once he pulls away, a knowing grin on his face. "I'm glad Rocco finally brought you home."

"Oh, um...it's not actually like that," I stammer, a hot flush creeping up the sides of my neck. "I only came because—"

"She does volunteer work at the shelter where we got Stoli 2." Rocco crosses the room to face his dad. "She missed him, so I offered to bring her over so she could see him." He shrugs. "No big deal. You don't have to get out the baby pictures or anything like that. We're just friends."

*Just friends.* Fuck. I won't lie. Hearing Rocco speak those words so casually...damn, the impact was like a knife stabbing my heart. I focus my attention on Stoli 2 and stroke his back as he lounges at my feet.

I know what this is. I'm not an idiot.

And a few months ago, it wouldn't have bothered me at all.

But now?

Things have changed.

I've changed.

I want more. And I want it with him.

I've tried to ignore it, but the reality is right there, taking a bite out of me every time I try to deny the truth to myself.

I was out of line last night. The alcohol made me crazy and

jealous, and I screwed things up big time. I'd been playing him for months, teasing him and taunting him, throwing out so many mixed signals, I even started to confuse myself. Did I really expect that he'd take the bait when I finally threw myself at him?

The guy clearly thinks I'm off my nut. Maybe that's the real reason why he wanted me to come here. He didn't trust me to be by myself, especially after finding me at the shelter dangling precariously over the brink of sanity.

He thought I crumbled in the wake of his rejection.

Little does he know how much worse I've had to deal with, how his rejection was only a tiny pin prick in comparison to the gutting I suffered eight years ago.

I manage a smile and nod at Antonio. "Rocco told me he was picking up Stoli 2, so I'm just along for the ride."

My eyes dart to Rocco's face almost as soon as the words tumble from my lips, betraying my mind and my heart. I want to look, but I'm so afraid to see...

I swallow hard as his eyes flicker over to mine, holding the same question that's on the tip of my tongue. The one I have to choke back.

Because speaking it would just make things worse.

As I said before, I'm not an idiot.

And this can't work because *I* don't work anymore.

I'm broken.

So, whatever I think I may want is irrelevant.

The shards of my former self won't let me be happy.

The memories of my past life, the terror I've experienced, the horrors I've committed...I can't seek comfort with anyone.

I'm on my own, an opinion my father seems to share as well since he's gone more than he's here...literally *and* figuratively.

So *just friends* is as good as I'm going to get because anything more just isn't possible.

Happily ever after isn't in my future.

Mine is a cold, solitary one permeated with the stench of death.

It's my fate, one I've prepared for. It's what I'm good at. And I won't stop until I find those who stole the lives of Mom and Lili.

I tear my eyes away from Rocco's. He was smart to push me away last night. What the hell could I possibly offer him? He is surrounded by love and a family who welcomes him with open arms. When his dad hugged me, I fought the urge to weep. It felt so nice to be wanted.

He doesn't need my level of crazy in his life.

That's the answer to your question, Rocco.

And it answers mine, too.

Lindy comes running back into the kitchen not a second too soon, and I grab my glass of wine and take a large gulp to dissolve the lump lodged in my throat. She waves a couple of leather-bound books in her hand, grinning from ear to ear. "I know you said we didn't need to get out the baby pictures, *but...*"

I cover my mouth to snort back a loud chuckle when I see Rocco's face drop to the tile floor. "Lindy, are you serious? Come on!"

Allegra rushes over with her own glass of wine and plops into the chair next to me. "Oh yes! What a great idea, Lindy! Rocco, come sit next to me!" She smacks the seat of the chair next to her, and Rocco's face twists into a grimace as he collapses into it.

Lindy hovers over me and flips open the first album, her excited and incessant chatter filling me with sadness. God, she's so much like Lili. So full of life and enthusiasm. Hell, she even sounds like Lili.

Her long hair spills over her shoulder, and I catch a whiff of mint.

Lili's favorite body wash was eucalyptus mint.

Lindy's hot pink fingernails point out various faces that swim on the pages in front of me.

It was Lili's favorite choice of polish color.

I tug on the ends of my hair. Why is this happening? Is this some sick and twisted way the universe is taunting me, today of all days?

The faces swim faster as tears pool in my eyes as Lindy points out different people and family events.

My breath catches as Lindy's fingers flip pages.

Or...

Maybe it's the universe giving me a little piece of my life back, just for a little while reminding me that I'm not alone after all. Stoli 2 chooses that very second to leap into my lap and nestle against me. I look up and catch Rocco staring at me. His brow furrows, and he knows something is wrong. But I don't let the tears fall. Instead, I smile.

I actually smile.

And something deep inside tells me that maybe...just maybe...I'm going to be okay after all.

It's an odd feeling, one I've never quite experienced before.

Perhaps the universe is sending me a different message this year, one that isn't laced with thoughts and plans for revenge. Maybe this year, it has a deeper meaning...hope, faith, happiness...things I figured were long buried in the past.

The possibility doesn't fix me. It doesn't instantly glue my heart back together. It doesn't make me forget.

But it does awaken something in me that I thought flickered out a long time ago — the desire to be happy. I'd squelched it, not believing I deserved it. I'd been spared for some unknown reason, and I didn't stop the disaster from occurring. I could have done something. I could have helped them. And Papa...it's not like he ever really made an effort to engage with me as a parent after everything happened. We both kind of retreated into our own anger, regret, and sadness, living together, working together, but never really connecting.

Surviving that horror was like my own personal hell on Earth. I felt like living was punishment for not taking action. And then I spent the next eight years trying to make up for it, trying to punish people who'd crossed us the same way I'd been punished — by taking everything from them.

Deep down, I'd hoped Papa would finally figure out why I'm so good at my job, why I'm so intent on making people pay for their wrongs. That maybe he'd respond to my blood-soaked cry for help because Ivanovs don't just break down and lose their shit when things get tough. They channel that emotion into other, more productive things like killing that slimy bastard Ian Raines as punishment for screwing us over and stealing what's ours.

Dammit! I need my brain to stop functioning for just a few minutes so I can pull myself back together.

Maybe I need some more wine. Whatever I'd gulped down made my insides feel nice and toasty. A little more will take the edge off and numb my thoughts, at least temporarily. That's all I really want for my birthday this year. A break from my inner turmoil.

And oh, yeah. Maybe an acknowledgement from my father who has yet to so much as send me a text. I take a deep breath, my fingers closing around the wine glass stem. My eyes have been focused on the photos and so are everyone else's, so at least my little silent breakdown went unnoticed.

I point to a picture of three little dark-haired boys on a beach and sniffle-smile at the same time, praying I don't look like an emotional basket case in front of Rocco's family. The tears are in check, but I'm a little nervous that they may go rogue at any second.

I need a diversion, and I think I found it.

"These little boys..." I murmur.

Rocco chuckles. "Me, Max, and Nico, at Nico's grandparents' house on the shore." He turns to his father. "Grandpa Vito's famous summer barbecue. How many of us were able to fit in that place? I remember all of us kids were piled on top of each other on the living room floor. Jesus, there must have been, what, twenty of us?"

Allegra smiles. "Those were fun days. And for as big as that house was, Vito and Lou managed to fill it every weekend. And the food!"

Antonio chuckles. "It never ended! Course after course after course. If you didn't go to sleep feeling like you were going to pop, Grandma Lou would have made you eat more. Nobody in her house ever went hungry."

I run my fingers over the picture. "It sounds like you had a lot of fun growing up with Max and Nico."

"Yeah..." Rocco's voice trails off. "We did."

Antonio claps Rocco on the back. "Let's set the table for dinner. The pizza should be here soon."

I grab my wine glass and stand up, backing away from the table. "Looks like you need a refill," Allegra says, holding out the wine bottle.

"Yes. It really is delicious." She fills my glass with the magical red liquid that has the power to relax my mind and body like nothing else. It amazes me how vodka has zero effect on me, regardless of how I guzzle it like water. But this wine...it actually calms me. Blunts the need for revenge yet fires up my libido at the same time.

Magic juice, I'm telling you.

I think I need to hit a liquor store on my way home.

Rocco finishes putting out forks and knives and looks over at me. I don't make eye contact. I don't need to. I can feel the heat of his gaze on me, searing my insides. Butterflies swarm in my belly, agitated by the wine. I want to look, but I force myself to focus on Allegra. She asks me about work at the shelter, and I tell her about the animals and where they come from, how they found their way to our temporary home. I prattle on for a few minutes until the doorbell chimes and everyone cheers and Stoli 2 dashes over to the front door, barking like he knows what's waiting outside.

Pizza is here!

I don't want pizza. I just want more wine. My mind gets

fuzzier by the minute, and I just want to hold on to this feeling for a little longer. Pizza will just soak it all up.

Allegra rushes to the front door to help Antonio with the boxes with Stoli 2 hot on her heels, and Lindy grabs a pile of napkins, placing them at our spots around the table.

Rocco walks over to me, a crooked smile on his face. "Isn't this fun?"

I nod. "It really is," I whisper. "Thank you for bringing me."

He nods, placing a hand on the small of my back. His fingertips scorch my skin through the thick velour, and those damn butterflies are at it again. "Sit down," he murmurs against my ear. "I think you should eat something."

"I was thinking the same thing," I whisper in an unintentionally flirty tone, gazing up at him through my lashes. Oh, crap. Here we go. Maybe the pizza isn't such a bad idea after all. Remember last night? Let's not have a replay of that disaster!

He furrows his brow, and I clear my throat, reading his expression loud and clear. Like I didn't already get the message last night. So many messages. My mind can't keep track of them all right now. Because of the wine. Yes, that's it. I'll just blame it on the vino. "You know, because of the drinking. On an empty stomach." I run a hand through my hair, turning away from him as heat floods my cheeks. *Keep it in check, Kat!*

Stoli 2 trots back into the kitchen and sits right at Antonio's feet as he opens that first box. The smell of melted cheese and sauce makes my mouth water, and judging from Stoli 2's reaction, he's on the same page as me.

The first bite singes the roof of my mouth, but my God, it tastes amazing.

Pizza can make almost anything better.

I inhale that first slice, and when I'm on my third, I raise my eyes to see Rocco staring at me again. I swallow hard, forcing the large bite of cheese and bread down my throat. He grins at me. "I think you've just soaked up your last months' worth of booze," he murmurs so only I can hear.

I snicker, covering my mouth with a napkin, trying not to spew sauce all over the table.

"She's got a good appetite." Allegra nods with a smile. "When I first saw you, I was afraid you'd be one of those girls who turns her nose up at anything that isn't a salad."

I wipe my lips and smile. "Nope. Pizza is my favorite. I could eat a whole pie by myself." I wink at Lindy. "And I have, too. More times than I'd like to admit."

"Girl's full of surprises," Rocco mutters, shaking his head and finishing the last half of his slice in one bite.

"Rocco!" Allegra chides. "You're going to choke!"

"Mnph. Itffohood." Rocco somehow manages to smile at his mother while he chomps away.

"You're disgusting." Lindy snorts, patting her slice with a napkin to mop up the excess oil.

I giggle as he leans over his sister, his mouth hanging open. She shrieks and pushes him away. "Gross! You are so freaking immature!"

Rocco doubles over with laughter as his mother rolls her eyes and lets out an exasperated sigh. "Kat, is dinner this eventful at your house?"

And just like that, all the air is sucked from the room. The pizza I'd just scarfed sits in my stomach like a concrete block, and my throat tightens. I clutch my neck, unable to breathe. Rocco and his father exchange a quick look...what the hell did it mean? Rocco puts a hand on my back. "Are you okay?"

I nod, my eyes filling with tears. "Something...went down the wrong pipe," I rasp. "I just need...a minute."

"Okay, dear." Allegra stands up and points to the hallway. "The powder room is just outside the kitchen. Do you want some water?"

I wave my hand. "No, thanks," I croak, rushing out of the room. Stoli 2 runs after me like he knows what's about to happen and wants to comfort me. Little does he know that he's exactly what I need right now. I find the small room, flip open the light, and lock myself and the dog inside before I finally let the tears flow. I wrap my arms around Stoli 2 and press my head against his, crying like I've just lost my best friend forever.

Oh, yeah.

I did.

## Chapter Fourteen
# ROCCO

"Can someone please tell me what just happened?" Mom whispers. "Did I say something wrong?"

I clap my hand against my forehead and let out a deep sigh. "No, you couldn't possibly know."

Dad puts an arm around Mom's shoulders. "It's not your fault. Kat has just had..." He looks at me. "A difficult life. Let's just leave it at that, okay?"

Mom has obviously heard this excuse plenty of times in the past, but it's new for Lindy. And unfortunately for me, the kid doesn't know when to quit.

"What happened?" she hisses. "Something with her family? Is someone sick? Or dead? Why can't you—?"

"Look, it's not something we can talk about, especially now." I run a hand through my hair and stand up, pacing around the island. How the hell am I going to handle this? How much longer am I going to be able to keep this secret from her?

Dad grabs my arm and pulls me into his office, leaving Mom and Lindy guessing about what the hell happened to Kat. "Listen, you can't say anything. You know that."

"I know." I trace my finger along the wood grain on his desk. "She has no clue that I know...anything."

"It has to stay that way. You're in enough trouble now that you're on their radar. You know what Viktor will do if he finds out you opened your mouth."

"Part of me doesn't even care anymore. There are plenty of people ready to pop me, why not add him to the list?" I press my fingers against my temples. "Goddammit! I hate that Vito roped me into this."

"That's your own fault." Dad lifts an eyebrow. "If I'd known the shit you were pulling behind everyone's' backs, I'd have straightened you out myself. You got yourself into this mess, and there wasn't anything I could do to stop it."

"I know!" Christ, it's on the tip of my tongue to tell him why I did it, why it wasn't because I was some prick out to screw over the family. But I keep it to myself. It's nobody's damn business. And for everything I stand to lose, I'd do it again in a hot second if it would bring my grandma peace of mind.

So, yeah. I'm prepared to deal with the consequences. I don't regret what I did at all.

And it might get me killed, but screw it. My conscience is clear.

"First thing tomorrow after dropping us off at the airport, you need to get your ass up to that farm and stay put until this situation is handled."

My mouth drops open. "How did you—?" And then I realize for the umpteenth time how shit works with the Salesis. "Joe told you."

"Of course he did." Dad rolls his eyes. "He wouldn't have let me leave the state without telling me the plan. I may be out of the game, but I'm still part of the family. And they're trying to protect you."

"Yeah, well, according to Viktor, the place isn't so safe anymore. That's why I'm still here. He said the location has been compromised."

Dad lets out a deep sigh. "I was afraid that might happen. Does anyone know how?"

"Who the hell knows? I mean, how it got out is a shock to me since Nico's lips are tighter than a duck's ass when it comes to 'family business'."

"Well, you know they're watching. I trust them with my life and the lives of my family, Rocco."

I'm quiet for a minute because there's still one thing that gnaws at me, a question nobody will answer, and I need to know the answer. "Dad, why did they spare Kat? Nobody called the cops after her mom and sister were killed, there was no rush to finish them off and escape. It doesn't make sense. If those assholes wanted revenge, why didn't they kill her, too?"

Dad looks at me for a long minute. "Because they need her, son. She's the only leverage they have left."

"What are you talking about? Leverage for what?"

Dad sighs. "We don't have a lot of time. She's going to come out, and you—"

"Screw that!" I whisper-shout. "That sonofabitch Nico has been holding out on me, telling me the littlest dipshit details about this whole clusterfuck, feeding me crumbs when my ass has the big red target on it. So, you'd better tell me what I need to know, Dad."

"The only thing you need to know is that Nico and his dad are all over this. They need you to watch over Kat while they handle the people who put the hit on Kat's mom and sister. You did your time in California, and now they have to handle the rest."

"No." I grit my teeth. "There's more to it. Tell me what it is!"

"Rocco, I'm trying to help—"

"Tell me!"

Dad slowly nods. "Fine. Not too long ago, Kat made a visit to a man named Ian Raines. Diamond dealer slash drug dealer. He'd fucked Viktor over, stole from him. Partnered with the Cinques because he needed a bailout. They used him as bait, knowing Kat would go after him, just like she has with every scumbag who has crossed her father over the past eight years. That's her MO, and they know it."

"Okay, so..." I fist my hair. "She killed him? Why is that bad? He deserved it."

"Yes, but it puts Viktor in a vulnerable spot."

"I don't get it." Jesus Christ, why is this so fucking murky? I didn't even drink that damn wine, and somehow, I'm still missing the big picture here. "What the hell does this have to do with me and the horse farm?"

I hear the bathroom door creak open. "Fast, Dad. No more games. Tell me what I need to know!"

"Viktor made a lot of enemies when he first came over from Russia. People didn't like the way he did business, and he was violent. Very violent. He killed a lot of people, stole a lot from the competition. And he made a name for himself. He was feared, until Xiomar Cinque rose up in power. He had a lot of connections in Mexico and wanted to bury Viktor. Drug and human trafficking were the big moneymakers and whoever won the battle would collect big time."

This mafia history lesson is making my temples pound. "Let's get to it, Dad. I've aged about ten years waiting for you to make your point."

"The point is, the Cinques put the hit on Viktor's family to scare him, to make him stand down, to chase him out of California...whatever the hell they needed him to do in order for them to rule the west coast."

"It doesn't explain why Kat is still alive."

"Kat is their insurance. They kept her alive because if Viktor went after them, they'd take her out, too. That's why he came out here and hooked up with the Salesis. Back then, his businesses were as dead as his family. He needed another lifeline, which is why he picked up with Vito. And the Cinques agreed to leave him alone as long as he left them alone and stayed on this coast." Dad sighs and sits in a leather recliner. "But Kat...Kat's the enforcer. And as time went on, she took a lot of risks going after her father's enemies. To her, if anyone crossed him, it was a betrayal and required extreme punishment."

"By death."

"Yes. But Raines was used to bait her. The Cinques knew she'd go after him because of what he'd done to her father. They tracked her."

"But they didn't kill her. Why?"

"That's the part we still don't know." Dad sweeps a hand over his head. "Or, at least, I don't know."

"Jesus Christ," I moan. "Why the fuck is everything on lock down all the time?"

"This is our life, Rocco. There are always a lot of unknowns."

"Yeah, I didn't sign up for this crap," I mutter.

Dad stands up and puts his hands on my shoulders. "Be careful, son."

"I'll be fine. Are you gonna be okay with Mom and Lindy?"

Dad nods. "Yes. Don't worry about us. The Salesis have people down there. We won't be alone. They'll be watching Grandma's house and anyone coming near it."

"I feel like a sitting duck. This really sucks."

"I know it does." He pulls me in for a bear hug and squeezes tight. "But it's only temporary. Talk to Nico."

"I've been trying," I grumble.

Dad claps me on the back. "You know he's going to take care of things. I love you, son. Always remember that."

I feel like I'm about to do the death row walk and it's damn unsettling. I needed to know what he just told me, but fuck, I didn't want to hear any of it. I figured once we knew who killed Kat's mom and sister, we could just take them out and be done with it. But shit has gone sideways...and then upside down and inside out. There's a reason why they haven't popped Kat. Viktor knows that reason, not that he'd ever tell me. And I don't want to wait around to find out.

Something big is gonna happen. That's why they haven't gotten to us yet.

If they wanted us dead, we'd already be fish food at the bottom of the Hudson River.

They want us alive. For now.

*Nico, what the hell are you doing to get me out of this mess?*

I pull open the door and walk into the hallway, hearing soft giggles and voices from the kitchen. The bathroom door is open, and the room is empty. Stoli 2 lets out a loud bark and comes running out of the kitchen, jumping on me. I ruffle the hair on his head. "You ready to go home, buddy?"

I walk into the kitchen, trying to forget what Dad just told me. It makes my stomach turn, but hey, it's the life. Mom and the girls are still flipping pages of the album. Kat looks up at me and her lips curl into a smile.

"You wanna go?" I ask.

She nods. "Okay."

"Oh, by the way, I left you a present at your place." Lindy grins, running over to me and giving me a big hug. "Don't eat it all in one night, okay?"

"Thanks, Lin." I squeeze her hard. "Be good, okay? I'll see you in the morning."

We say our goodbyes, and a few minutes later, Kat, Stoli 2, and I are in my car. My house is only about ten minutes away. Kat is quiet — studying her nails, toying with the drawstring on her pants, tugging on her hair — anything to keep her hands occupied and her mouth closed. I don't press because at this point, I don't even know what to say.

How much of what my dad just told me does she know? She'd been told the murders were at the hands of druggies looking for quick cash. Does she suspect something else? Did she know about Raines? Is that why she went after him? She's not stupid. She wouldn't just swallow bullshit without checking into it first.

And looking at those pictures...fuck. That had to hurt. But Mom and Lindy had no idea. They were just trying to be welcoming. They were excited I'd brought home a girl, but they have no clue what she's been through and what evidently is staring her in the face.

"Your family is so wonderful," she says, a tiny smile on her face. "You're really lucky."

"Thanks," I say, maneuvering my car into the driveway. I pull up to the back door and step on the brake. "We're really close. I'm sorry if they, ah, got a little too excited that I brought you home. I know they can be a little overwhelming."

She shakes her head. "No, not at all. I just...it's been a tough day. But being around them...and you...made it better."

I grin. "We aim to please." I push open the door, jog around the car, and pull open her door. She slides out with Stoli 2 right behind her. He runs around us in little circles, his tongue hanging out of his mouth. I've never seen Kat so happy. He jumps into her arms and she hugs him tight around the neck.

She needed this.

I take a quick look around, partly expecting someone to jump out of the bushes, but thankfully, nobody does. I unlock the door and let them in, shutting and locking the door behind us. I let out a relieved breath. We made it through another day.

But who knows what tomorrow will bring?

The rich scent of chocolate fills the place, and I smile. Lindy's specialty. God, I love that kid. She's so good to her big bro.

"Hey, Kat," I say, walking into the kitchen. Her back is to me, and it looks like she already found the large frosted cake sitting on the counter. "You hungry? My sister's an awesome baker, and—"

My next words are interrupted by a loud sob. Kat turns around slowly, her teeth chattering. Tears stream down her face, and her shoulders quiver. She covers her face with her hands, Stoli 2 whimpering at her feet. "I c-can't. I'm s-sorry. It's just t-too...t-too..." Her voice, thick with sadness, trails off, and the hysterics take over. I wrap my arms around her, and she collapses against me all over again, crying like her heart is breaking.

I rub my hands up and down her back, pressing my face against her hair. She hugs me tighter, her breathing labored as the sobs quake her body.

We stand like that for several minutes. Feels like hours. I have so many questions. What in the fuck does this all mean? First the shelter, then my parents' house, now this? For a while, I'd known exactly what to expect from Katarina Ivanov, but between last night and today, I'm completely confused about who this woman really is, plain and simple.

But what's worse is that I know things that can answer her questions. I have information that can at least give her some closure.

The problem is, if I open my mouth, my nuts will be in a vise, one that will crush them into oblivion.

That's the one thing I'm pretty clear on. Nico has at least set that expectation for me.

So, I keep quiet, as usual. Even though my gut clenches with each sob that makes her body shudder against me.

I have a choice. I can give her the closure she needs and help her heal.

Or I can kiss my ass goodbye.

It's pretty cut and dry.

She finally pulls away and wipes her eyes. The sadness reflected in the depths makes my gut twist like a pretzel.

"Do you want some water?" I ask, smoothing her hair away from her face with one hand, my other one still on the small of her back. As hard as it is to look at her without admitting what I've seen and heard, I'm still mesmerized by the heavy emotion scrawled all over her beautiful face. The fact that this woman can vacillate between cold assassin and emotional train wreck in a hot second boggles my mind, and Christ only knows how she'd react if she knew the shit looping through my mind right now.

"Yes, please." She bites her lower lip. "But don't let me go, okay?"

We move together toward the fridge, and I pull it open with

one hand, grabbing a bottle from the shelf. I let the door slam shut and hand her the bottle. I keep my arms wrapped around her as she twists off the cap and takes a long sip. She slips the bottle under my arm and places it on the counter before resting her head against my chest again. Her breathing has finally calmed, and I can feel her heartbeat thumping against my chest. I drop my head on top of hers, stroking the back of her hair until she's ready to speak.

I swallow hard, past the golf ball-sized lump in my throat.

I want to comfort her. I want to take away her pain. I want so much, dammit.

But if she knew what I'd done, she'd hate me.

Hell, she might even kill me.

"Can we sit down?" she whispers.

"Yeah, of course." I lead her into the living room and over to the couch, where she drops into the plush cushion. I sink next to her and she slides over, plastering herself against me. It's hard to ignore the effect of her body pressed against mine, and fuck me, I'm a sicko for even thinking that. But it doesn't stop the blood from rushing to my groin. And it doesn't prevent my pulse from throbbing against my neck. And it sure won't keep my fingers from twitching, desperate to trace a path across her soft, smooth skin.

"I love chocolate cake," she says in a tearful voice. "I mean, I used to love it. Now, I can't even stand the smell of it." Loud sniffle. "My mom used to make me and my twin sister a chocolate cake every year on our birthday. She knew how much we loved them." Kat takes a long, unsteady breath. "The last one she made was on our sixteenth birthday, eight years ago."

I tighten my arms around her, pressing my lips together, waiting for her to continue with the story I already know too well, barely breathing...

"That was the day she and my sister were murdered." Her voice quivers, but she continues with her gut-wrenching story. "The cops said it was drug addicts who were looking to make some quick cash. They broke into my house, killed Mom and Lili..." She pulls herself off of me, her dark hair soaked with tears and matted to the sides of her face. "They killed Stoli, our dog, too. But not me. They knocked me out before they left, but they didn't hurt me at all. I never understood why. Why did I survive? When I woke up, there were cops, paramedics, and neighbors swarming the place. I saw Mom and Lili lying next to each other and there was blood...so much blood..." Her eyes brim with tears, and she shakes her head. "Those bastards let me live, and every day since then, I wish they'd killed me, too."

"No, Kat," I whisper, my voice thick. "Don't say that."

She nods, the tears flowing down her cheeks. "I mean it," she murmurs. "They're gone, and I'm here, all alone. I miss them so much. It never gets better or easier. That's what everyone says will happen over time, but it doesn't. It hurts just as much now as it did then. And my dad...he doesn't care about me. Especially today."

"What's today?" I swipe away the tears with my thumb and forefinger.

"It's my birthday. The anniversary of their death."

And to celebrate, we have Lindy's cake taunting us from the kitchen island. "And Lindy's cake brought it all back. I'll get rid of it right now." I make a move to pull myself off the couch, but Kat's fingers grip my wrist.

"Don't you dare," she said. "Lindy would be so upset. She made it for you."

"I'm more concerned about you than my stomach."

"I appreciate it. Nobody has said that to me in a really long time."

"That they pick you over dessert?"

"That they pick me at all." Her lips curl into a half-smile. "So, thanks."

"I'd always pick you." Oh, shit. Those words sneaked out before I could gulp them back in.

She tilts her head to the side. "That's good to know.

Although I was pretty sure after last night, you'd feel the exact opposite way. You were right, too. I was out of line. It's just a really hard time for me. Every year, I relive that day, those moments of terror." She shakes her head. "And I do it alone. My dad...he disappears at the same time every year to drown his sorrows in vodka at the same hotel we stayed at when we were kids and came to New York for a fun family weekend. Fun family weekends didn't happen often because of his work. I guess he goes there because he knows he'll never have another one again, and it's a reminder of everything he lost." She sniffles. "And I haven't gotten so much as a *How are you?* text on this day for the past eight years."

"I hate hearing that," I mutter. What a scumbag. Holding out on his only surviving daughter for almost a decade, convincing her the cops were right about drug addicts killing her mom and sister when it was all his fucking doing...his business, his enemies. He did shit that destroyed his family. For all of this time, he's left Kat in the dark, by herself, to deal with the demons who keep haunting her.

And now I'm just one more person who's feeding into the lies.

A sharp ache assaults my heart at the realization. "Kat, I...I really am so sorry."

"Thanks," she whispers. "You know, I've never told anyone about what happened to them. I mean, Shaye knows they died, but I never told her any more than that. She's probably the only friend I really have."

My brow furrows. "Hey, what about me?"

She taps a fingertip to her tear-streaked cheek. "I don't know. I haven't quite figured you out yet."

"Yeah, well, same here. I thought you were some insane, twisted bitch with a black soul and huge chip on her shoulder."

"And now you think differently?"

I smirk. "Not really. I just have the backstory now."

"Asshole."

"Crazy bitch."

She chuckles and smacks my chest. I grab her wrist before she has time to jerk it away. She loses her balance and falls against me, her lips so close to mine I can almost taste them.

"Are you planning to let me go?" she whispers, breathless.

"No," I rasp, my heart thumping against my ribs. "I'm not. If that's okay with you."

She nods, her eyes wide and fixed on mine. "It is..." She dips her head the slightest bit, hovering her mouth over mine. For a few agonizing seconds, I wonder if she's debating her next move, praying she gives in, desperate to feel her soft lips crush against mine. "But I don't want you to do this because you feel sorry for me. I want you to do it because you want to. Because you want...me."

My throat is so tight I can barely take in oxygen. A knot of tears catches in my throat. Jesus Christ, what is wrong with me? Am I really so caught up in her hell that I'm about to lose my shit right now? I want to beat the shit out of that bastard father of hers for doing this to her in the first place. Leaving her all alone, year after year, nursing the guilt and regret over something he caused because he was a greedy, selfish bastard. He lost so much, but he still has Kat. Can't he see that? Doesn't he know how fucking amazing she is?

But as amazing as she is, she's still lost. And sad. And dammit, she needs to know that someone still cares...that someone still loves her.

I pull her against me, sliding one of my hands down the side of her face. "I do want you, Kat. I've wanted you for so fucking long, more than you'll ever know."

Her lips curl upward. "Good," she murmurs, running a hand through my hair and around the back of my neck. Her warm breath feels like feathers against my face, and even though I want to devour her, I need to look at her. She's so beautiful, but vulnerable, more than I ever imagined. I'd thought she had it all together. The Russian Ice Queen who was a better sniper than anyone in our family...in any family, for that matter. I'd always suspected there was something buried behind that icy façade, but I never thought it'd break her. She's always been so strong, so focused, so controlled.

But not today.

Because she's still human. She's not some fembot that I pegged her for. She's dealing with a mess of emotions I'll bet she has no clue how to process, shit she's been plagued with for eight years.

And today she finally let someone in.

So, yeah, I want to look at her. She's finally letting me see her for who she really is — her fears, her grief, her desires. I don't want to miss any of it. I could stare at this woman forever.

I *want* to stare at her forever...

I lean up from the couch and pull her into my lap, tangling my fingers in her hair. She tips her head back, her eyes closed, lips parted. I bury my head in her sweet-smelling neck, my tongue tracing a path over her flushed skin. I nuzzle her ear with my teeth, and a tiny mewl escapes her lips. "That feels so good," she whispers.

"Just wait."

"The suspense is killing me." Her half-hooded blue eyes sends a jolt straight to my cock, and I don't know how much longer I'm gonna be able to resist stripping her down and throwing her on my bed. But I'm trying to go slow. She needs to feel like this means something, that it's not a pity fuck.

But telling her the truth, that I can't stop thinking about her, that I've thought of nothing else since she came into my life, that sending her away last night was torture...I don't know if she's ready to hear all of that.

To her, last night was another rejection from someone who supposedly cared about her. I'm part of the reason —at least a small part — why she came apart today.

Knowing that makes my stomach clench, but that's why I need to take my time with her. This is real for me, and I don't know if I'm gonna get another shot to show her how I feel. Maybe this is what she needs right now. To feel wanted and protected. But tomorrow, who knows?

I know how I'll still feel.

Things might look different to her the morning after, though.

I chase that thought out of my mind. One shot is what I have. After that, it's up to her.

I pull her tight, my mouth crashing against hers. I force open her lips with my tongue and plunge into her heat. Our tongues coil, our teeth crack against each other, and the electricity between us is so powerful, it damn-near sizzles all of my brain cells at once.

Our mouths are frenzied, as if parting would drain our bodies of whatever we need to survive...namely, each other. We breathe our desire into each other with every second that passes, and now that I've had a taste of this woman, I know I'm ruined for anyone else.

I lift myself off of the couch with her secure in my arms. But I don't break the kiss. I need that connection. I can't function without it. I'd fantasized about it for so long, and the reality? Fucking blows away everything I imagined.

Luckily, there's a bedroom on the first floor.

I somehow manage to find my way into the bedroom off the living room. I twist the knob with one hand and kick open the door. I don't bother with the lights. The hardwood floor creaks beneath my feet, and I hope I'm getting close to the bed. The closer I get to the bed, the faster I can get her naked. My cock is about to bust through my jeans right now, and if I don't get there soon—

*Crash!*

"Ahhh!" I swing around, collapsing onto the mattress and pulling Kat on top of me. The pain is so intense, tears spring to my eyes. "Goddammit!"

"What happened?" she whispers, breathless.

"My fucking toe. I slammed it into the bed frame." I clench

my teeth. Real smooth. Nobody can say foreplay with me isn't eventful.

"Well, maybe I can give you something else to think about." Kat leans back on her heels and unzips her sweat jacket, taking her sweet time to expose those perfect tits spilling out of a black lacy bra. Her lips lift into a sexy grin, and the toe pain that was just shooting through my foot and up my ankle immediately dissipates.

"It's starting to feel a little bit better," I say, winking at her. "But I think I may need more of a distraction, something that's really gonna chase away the pain."

Kat's jacket falls behind her on the bed, and she crawls closer. Her hair swings around her face, the ends tickling my chin. Her blue eyes are dark with lust as she brings herself to a kneeling position and loops her fingers into the waistband of her pants, pushing them down over her hips to reveal a black lacy thong that matches her bra.

Fuck me, I want to bite it off of her with my teeth...

She slides off the thong, one leg at a time, her eyes never moving from my face. The pain has definitely eased up in my toe, and the ache has pretty much settled in my balls.

"Is that better?" she asks, a coy smile on her face.

"Well," I say, pretending to think about it. "It's better, but I'm still not there yet. I think you need to come up with something else, something that's gonna cure me for good."

She leans over me, one hand on either side of my shoulders. "I think I need your help with this last part. Your hands didn't slam into the bed frame, did they? Maybe they can get in on the action, too."

I love this whole cat and mouse thing we've got going on. Kat, get ready to meet mouse. My dick is about to explode out of my pants, but I don't give a fuck. I love the torture. And I've waited for this for too long. There's no way I'm rushing any of it.

I loop my fingers around the front of her bra and flick it open, letting her breasts freely graze my chest. She shrugs out of it and slides herself against me, letting her lips graze my chin as she works her way up to my mouth. I reach my hands around her, fisting her hair as I devour her mouth like I'll never have this chance again.

And maybe I won't. But I'm not gonna think about that now. I don't care what happens tomorrow. I only care about what's happening right now, and it's more incredible than I ever imagined.

I kiss her long and hard, gasping for breath but not willing to break the connection between us. Her fingers fumble with my belt buckle, and I let out a low groan against her lips when her hand grasps my throbbing cock. She slides it up and down, stroking, pulling, and massaging the tip until I'm afraid I may blow my load from a hand job alone.

No way is that happening to me! Max already thinks I have a small dick, so yeah, I don't need him getting wind of me losing my shit as quick as a fifteen-year-old virgin.

I reach behind her and grab her ass, squeezing it and pressing her closer to me until she starts rubbing herself over my dick. I can feel how wet she is through the flimsy lace panties, and all I want is to tear them off and sink into her soft pussy. She breaks away from my lips for an agonizing second to pull my shirt over my head. Then she crawls away from me, a come-hither look on her face.

Fuck yeah, I'm ready to come.

Anywhere.

Any way.

Anyhow.

She pulls off my jeans and tosses them on the floor next to everything else we stripped off. I sit up and swing her around so she is flat on her back in the center of the bed. My dick is stiff as a corpse, but we've only just gotten started. He can hang in there a little longer. Okay, maybe hang is the wrong word since he's hard enough to gouge out someone's eye right about now.

He's not hanging.

He's at the ready.

Willing and able.

I run a hand down the front of her torso, over the indentations of muscle in her abs. I lean down and trace them with my tongue, my fingers working to peel the panties from her quivering body. I dip my head lower, breathing in her scent, letting it fuel my desire. I grip the sides of her hips and she tilts them upward for me. My tongue delves into her wet heat, making her gasp and thrust her hips harder against my mouth. Her fingers tangle in my hair, pulling it hard as I gently tease her clit with my teeth.

"Ahh! My God, that's amazing!" she whimpers. "More, more, holy shit! Don't stop!"

And I have no intention of doing that anytime soon.

I drink in her sweet juices, tremors quaking her body as I launch her into space once, twice, three times…who the fuck even knows? I'm not keeping track, but the deep gashes across my back tell me it's a record for her.

My dick is dripping on my leg, so ready to have his own fun right now, greedy bastard that he is.

Time escapes me. I'm drowning in this woman, and I don't give a damn what day, month, or year it is. I would be perfectly happy doing this for the rest of my life and forgetting all of the other bullshit that plagues me on a daily basis. Because she really is everything. She may not know it, and it'll kill me if she doesn't feel the same way, but for now, I can just pretend that she does. That this isn't another distraction for her. That it's deeper and means something.

Like she's in love with me, too.

But how stupid am I for even thinking that? She's got too much of her own shit to deal with. Falling in love with me probably isn't high on her priority list.

Especially when she finds out what I know and what I've kept from her.

There's a thought that can make my dick go limp faster than she can put me in another one of her famous chokeholds.

So I'm not gonna think about any of that, because my dick wants nothing more than to sink into her perfect pussy.

I've made him wait long enough.

I pull away, trying to catch my breath, and damn, the places where she lanced my back sting like a motherfucker. I think she drew blood on a few of them.

Totally worth it, though.

Her chest heaves as I crawl upward, taking my time to feel her bare skin against mine. I take her breasts into my mouth, one by one, my tongue and teeth teasing her nipples. She squeals and wiggles around underneath me, but I've got her pinned. She ain't going anywhere for the foreseeable future.

"You're incredible," she breathes against my ear, her teeth tugging on my earlobe. My cock thickens against her pussy, the head right there at her opening, so close to diving into her. "I want to feel you inside of me. Now."

"You're so bossy," I murmur, dropping kisses on her forehead, the tip of her nose, and each cheek. "Say the magic word."

"Pill." She lets out a soft giggle.

"Nice," I murmur. "I like that word. But I was thinking of a different one, one that begins with a 'p'."

"Oh, you mean...*penis*," she whispers, dragging her fingertips down the sides of my torso.

I let out a groan. "You're so bad, do you know that?"

She smirks. "Yep. But you love it."

"Fuck yeah, I do." I lower my hips, the head of my dick plunging into her slit. I let out a loud gasp in that second. I've fucked a lot of girls in my life, but it's never felt like this. Flames ignite in my groin, roaring through me, powering every thrust deeper into her wet heat. I drive into her, as far as I can. Her walls clench around me, squeezing my cock and urging it deeper. I pull out part way, rubbing my dick against her clit and then sinking back into her. She locks her ankles around my waist, keeping me deep inside of her. My gut clenches as I thrust long and hard, searching for the spot that's going to make her scream my name again...over and over...hopefully all night long and into tomorrow morning.

The nails are back in force, raking down my sides, causing such sweet agony as my body trembles against hers. Perspiration pebbles our skin. Our slick bodies slide against each other, legs and arms flailing around until we're completely entangled, knotted together like we'll never come undone.

Her breathing is labored, coming in short, sharp gasps, and I know she's close. "Go slow," she rasps. "Don't pull out. Oh my God! Just like that!"

I do exactly as she asks. My strokes are long and deep, and within seconds, her screams pierce the still air. I clutch her against me, pressing my forehead against hers.

I watch as her eyes squeeze shut, as her mouth stretches wide, begging me to come with her. I thrust a few more times, tremors rumbling through my entire body, preparing for the massive explosion that's about to rock my entire world. My stomach clenches as the orgasm blasts through my limbs until they are spent and limp as spaghetti noodles. I can't think. I can't speak. I can't hear. I can't breathe.

I've lost myself, and dammit, I don't think I ever want to be found.

Because I am consumed by this woman...utterly and completely...in every possible way.

I roll off of her and fling an arm over my face. "Wow."

"Yeah. Ditto." She lets out a deep sigh. "Now I get the whole joke about the spicy Italian sausage." A breathless giggle escapes from her lips.

"It's no joking matter," I respond in a serious voice.

"Clearly." Kat turns on her side and looks at me, a smile on her flushed face. "That was pretty otherworldly. I didn't know you had it in you."

"Um, I think we can both agree it was actually in *you*." I wink, tucking a loose strand of hair behind her ear.

"Mm-hm. And I'd like you to stick me with your sausage again."

"Good thing you know the magic word now."

"Who knew you were that easy?"

"Come on, I'm sure you've heard the rumors."

"Yes, but I didn't believe them."

"Well, make sure you tell everyone that the spicy Italian sausage ain't no urban legend, alright?" I pull her on top of me until our noses touch.

She grins. "Yeah, but then I'll have to fight off the girls who want to get a taste."

"Knowing you, that won't work out too well for them."

"No." She kisses my nose lightly, her eyes glimmering with a light I've never seen.

"Hey, by the way," I murmur. "Happy birthday."

Her lips stretch into a wide smile. "Thanks. I loved my present."

God, I am so crazy about this girl.

Fuck my life.

*Chapter Fifteen*

# KATARINA

I can't remember the last time I slept through the night without being tortured by the horrors of that day.

I can thank Rocco for that. Because of him, I never wanted to close my eyes. I didn't want our time together to end. And now, even as I crack open my eyes in the morning light streaming through the window shades, I know I have to move forward.

But all I want to do is hit the rewind button and relive those blissful hours on top of him, under him, in front of him, and a whole slew of other positions I haven't begun to catalog.

I've never felt so peaceful.

Or physically exhausted.

My limbs are wobbly like Jell-O, and if I try to swing my legs over the side of the bed, there's a good chance I'll collapse on the floor.

And I don't know that I'd be in any rush to get up.

I clutch the bedsheet up to my chin and let out a deep sigh, running my hand through my tangled mess of hair. I cringe. What the hell must I look like right now? I grab my cheeks and pinch them to bring some color into them since I must be as white as this sheet.

I flip over to find an empty spot next to me and my gut clenches.

Guys who don't wake up next to you are usually the ones who are ready to call you an Uber the second your eyes open.

I bury my face in his pillow and inhale his fresh and clean scent. I couldn't have read all of that wrong, right? It felt too real to be bullshit.

Or maybe it's just been long enough that I can't recognize the difference anymore.

"Goddammit!" I shout into the pillow, which comes out sounding more like "Mnhammit!"

The bedroom door creaks open, and Rocco peeks his head in, a smile plastered on his face.

"You called?"

I gasp and sit up, pulling the sheet over me. "Oh, I, um..."

"You know I already saw you naked, right?" he says, carrying a tray piled high with food over to the bed.

"Yes," I say in a small voice, clutching the sheet tighter.

"Just making sure you remember." He points to the dishes on the tray. "Hey, so I figured you might be hungry. I know you pretty much live on vodka and pizza, but you know, since it's breakfast, I thought we'd try something new."

"We tried a lot of new things last night." I raise my eyes up from the tray and tiny shivers shimmy across my bare skin when spots of red appear in his cheeks.

"And believe me, I'd like to try plenty more." He hands me a mug with steam rising out of it.

"Really?" I whisper. *Cool, Kat. Way to play hard to get.*

"Yeah," he says, leaning toward me and brushing his lips against mine. "That is, if you're down with it. You must have been some kinda gymnast in your past life or something." He lets out a low whistle and shakes his head.

I blow on the coffee and take a tiny sip. It scorches my esophagus and lands in my empty belly, heating me from the inside out. "I used to be a competitive gymnast. A long time ago."

"That explains a lot." Rocco smirks. "Who's the lucky boy?"

I giggle and look down at the tray of eggs, toast, fruit, bacon, breakfast sausages...I have to laugh at that one...and cereal. "How long did it take you to prepare this tray?"

"Long enough. Every second was worth it, though."

"You're sweet."

"You sound surprised."

I tilt my head. "Not surprised at you. More surprised at myself."

"Why? Never thought you'd score a catch like me who can cook and make your toes curl at the same time?"

I swat at his arm. "While that's definitely a feat, it's more about me opening up. I don't do that. And I don't do parents, either. But somehow you got me to do both. In one day. The worst day of every year." I shrug. "It's odd. For me."

"Do you feel better?" His dark eyes are so warm, so concerned, so...invested. He cares. Somebody actually *cares*.

I take a deep breath. Physically, hell yes! Delicious aftershocks rocked me to sleep last night, and the memories of Rocco's body, his hands, his mouth all over me...good God, it was every fantasy turned reality.

But emotionally?

The pain never goes away. I'll always carry the loss and everything that goes along with it. And being rejected by my father? Yeah, that still hurts like a bitch, too.

Yet something new has taken over my heart...something that, for the first time, can blunt the anguish.

The pain is still there, but there's less of it weighing me down. I feel lighter, like the burden of what I've carried with me for so long isn't quite as heavy.

Or dark.

And now there is a sliver of hope cutting through the murk.

A hint of what my future can become. A glimpse of who I want to be part of it.

"Yes." I grin and pick up a strawberry. "I do."

"Oh," he muses. "Okay, then."

"Why do you sound disappointed?" I pop the strawberry into my mouth.

Rocco shrugs and leans back on his elbows, the muscles in his chest tightening. "If you're feeling better, my job is done. You don't need me anymore."

I move the tray aside and drop the sheet before climbing on top of him. "You think that's all I wanted from you? Just some sex therapy?"

"You used me for the spicy Italian sausage, and now you don't need it anymore." He gives me the puppy dog eyes, and I let out a loud snicker.

"Don't you worry. I am in no way finished with it." I drop little kisses down the front of his abdomen and spread his legs. "I'm starving, too. And I'd rather have you than anything else on that tray."

I drag my fingernails down his sides, and he jumps, letting out a loud shriek. My eyes widen. "Jesus, did that noise come out of you?"

"I'm ticklish," he says.

"You're serious?"

He nods. "Yep."

"And you scream like a bitch every time it happens?"

"Not something I'm proud of, but we all have our crosses to bear."

I look at him hard for a few seconds. "You know, the more I get to know you, the less I think of you as a mafia thug."

He chuckles. "Thanks. Except it doesn't really sound like much of a compliment."

I shake my head. "It's not."

"You're still turned on. Admit it."

"I am." I grin, wiggling my fingernails in front of his face.

"But if you shatter a window with those squeals, I'm outta here." I take his hand and slide it down the front of my torso. "Mm, I think I know what I want for breakfast."

He jumps on the bed and pulls me to a sitting position, the bed sheet falling around me. I pull off his t-shirt, and he shoves his sweatpants to his ankles, flinging them off foot by foot.

*Ruff! Ruff! Ruff!*

He groans. "Aw, Stoli 2, come on, dude! You can't cockblock me in my own house, man. Not cool!"

I reach over and grab a piece of bacon. His tail wags a mile a minute, his tongue hanging out of his mouth. I hand it to him and he snatches it in one bite. I look back at Rocco. "See? That was easy enough."

"Thank God I made sure to bring you a good selection of *meat*."

I reach my arms around him, straddling my legs on either side of him. His lips crush against mine, his hands roaming down my back and over my ass. He lifts me so I'm in his lap, the head of his dick sliding against my pussy. Tingles erupt in my belly as he presses into me. I clench my teeth, throwing back my head as he thrusts into me, gripping me tight.

He presses his fingertips into my back as I bounce up and down on his cock. He stretches me wide, making me squeal every time he hits my spot, and my God, it feels fucking amazing. I want to scream and cry at the same time, it's that good.

He pulls away from my mouth, a sly grin on his face. "Turn around," he murmurs, twisting a lock of my hair around his finger.

Oh, *yes*!

I rotate my body and lower myself onto his throbbing cock, letting him fill me. "Oh my God," I whisper, my pulse ready to explode out of my neck. With one hand, he uses his fingers to stroke my clit as he fucks me long and hard. Each thrust makes me gasp. I clench my muscles tight around him, forcing him deeper with every push and pulse. He grabs my breasts with his free hand, kneading them with more and more force as his strokes get deeper and faster. His lips scorch the skin along the back of my neck and my breath hitches, catching a scream before it gathers the power to explode out of my mouth.

I press my hands against his, working my own clit through his fingers. My pussy spasms out of control as our bodies slap against each other, frenzied and fierce. Every cell in my body is electrified as the orgasm blasts through me, exploding with an erotic force I've never felt in my life.

"Holy fuck!" I gasp as he shudders against me with a loud groan. He buries his head in my neck, his stilted breath hot against my skin.

Minutes pass before we speak. I know I can barely find the words to express what in the hell he just did to me.

And judging by his silence, I'm hoping he feels the same way.

I collapse onto my stomach with him on top of me. I drop my head onto my arms, panting, my pussy still clenched tight around Rocco's cock. His hands graze my sides, making my skin prickle with renewed desire. This man. I just can't get enough. He drops his head on my shoulder, his lips tugging at my ear. We stay like that for a few moments, until he gently turns me over.

"Kat, this isn't…I'm not…" He pauses, mid-nuzzle, and my brow furrows.

My gut twists. There's a question in his gaze. Whether it's for me or for him, I'm not sure. "What's the matter?"

"Nothing. It's just that…" He pulls out of me and pulls me up onto his lap. "Last night, this morning…" He lets out an exasperated sigh and runs a hand through his hair. "Look, it means something to me. I didn't do it to make you feel better or to distract you."

My mouth drops open. Okay, not what I was expecting.

"When I said I wanted you, I meant it."

I stroke the side of his stubbled face, tracing over the outline of his lips before kissing them. "Oh, I know that."

"And when I tell you I love you, I mean it, too."

I kiss him again. "Okay."

Wait. *What?*

Cue the record scratch sound effect.

I recoil the second those words sink into my conscious. *Love?* Is he saying...? Did he say? No, he didn't tell me anything other than when he says it, he'll mean it. He didn't say he loves me.

His lips curl into a smile. "Yeah, that's right. I'm saying it. I love you. I've loved you from the second I saw you poke out that guy's eye with your shoe. I love your fire and your undying loyalty and your soul. Your sense of justice might be a little skewed, but hey, we can work on that." He presses his fingers over my chest, right over my heart. "I want this Kat. And I'll do anything to get it."

Tears sting my eyes. My lips crush against his, and I know for sure in that moment, my heart already been claimed.

I have no intention of ever taking it back.

## Chapter Sixteen
# ROCCO

"I love you, too," Kat whimpers, sniffing and wiping her eyes. "Wow. More tears. So much emotion. What would your assassin friends say?" I yelp as she wiggles her fingers under my armpit.

"You know what I'll do…" she threatens in a sing-song voice.

"Eh, you're all talk," I murmur, wrapping my arms tight around her.

"Wanna test me?"

"I can think of a lot of other things I want to do to you, and the only testing involved has to do with furniture and how hard I can make you come."

"I like the sound of that. Where should we start?"

*Ruff! Ruff! Ruff!*

More panting. More begging. More bacon, please!

I catch a glimpse of the clock on my night table and let out a loud groan. "Dammit, I didn't realize it was so late. I've got to get in the shower. I have to get my family to the airport for their flight." I hand Stoli 2 another slice of bacon.

"I'm amenable to that. I'd like to see how hard you can make me come in there."

"Mmm, multi-tasking. I fucking love it." I lace my fingers with hers. "Want to come along for the ride?"

She looks at me like I have five heads. "No way, dude. That would be hella awkward, don't you think? I mean, then they'd know I stayed over here."

"Which you did." I'm not following the logic.

"And that we had sex..."

"Which would make them really happy..."

She wrinkles her nose. "Oh my God, that's so creepy. Why would you say that?"

"Because they want us to get together. My mom and sister love you, just in case that didn't come over loud and clear. If they knew I slipped you the—"

"Don't say spicy Italian sausage again. I forbid it. Not when we're talking about your parents in the same sentence."

I smirk. "Okay, fine. Don't come."

She wiggles her fingers in front of my face. "You're tempting me..."

I smack her ass as she jumps off the bed. My ring tone blares from the kitchen, and I roll off the bed. "Get it nice and hot. I'll be right there."

"Don't keep me waiting too long. I may have to take things into my own hands."

"Oh, fuck yeah. Just save a little of the show for me." I pull on a pair of sweat pants, not really caring if I miss the call. If I do, I can find plenty of things to occupy me until whomever it is calls back.

She shrugs, giving me a look that makes my balls tight. I need to drive into that pussy again. Christ, I'm done for. One night, and I'm a goddamned addict.

I grab my phone and stab the Accept button. Jesus, it's about time.

Nico. He hates to be kept waiting.

How ironic that it's all he makes *me* do. I've only called and texted him about twenty times in the past twelve hours.

"Yeah," I bark into the phone, rubbing the back of my neck. I can hear the shower spray a few rooms away and my cock jumps as I picture Kat soaping up her tight body.

"Rocco, we have a problem."

Don't we always?

And why is it always *our* problem? Why can't it ever be everyone else's problem except mine?

"I know we do. I've been trying to get in touch with you about it, too. Maybe you saw all of the missed calls and messages?" I stretch my arms overhead and wince as my back cracks.

Occupational hazard. I've come close to ending up in traction more times than I care to count.

"I don't have time for your bullshit. Viktor's gone."

"What do you mean, gone?"

"Xiomar Cinque and his guys got into town a couple of days ago. I had a meeting with Viktor yesterday morning, after yours, and that was the last I've seen of him. I've tried calling, texting, everything except ask Kat."

"I wouldn't bother. He hasn't reached out to her, either," I mutter, scrubbing a hand down the front of my face.

"How do you know that?"

"Because she told me."

"Oh, yeah? When?"

"Um...last night. Before we had sex." I roll my eyes.

"For fuck's sake, Rocco. You know what we're up against here. I told you to keep an eye on her, not bang her!"

"Look, she's been with me since yesterday morning. She's safe. That's the important thing, right?"

Nico lets out a frustrated sigh. "Dude, keep it in your pants until we get this handled. You need to watch your ass. They're looking for you, too. Where is your family?"

"I'm getting ready to take them to the airport. They're heading down to Florida this afternoon."

"Okay, good. Get them out of here. We need to find a place for you guys."

"Yeah, thanks for letting me know the farm is out. I had to hear it from Viktor yesterday. I guess it was just one more thing you thought you'd keep close to the vest." I roll my eyes. "A little information is good sometimes, Nico. You know, like when my fucking life is at stake!"

"I told you to trust me, that I have everything under control. But right now, we need to get Kat out of the line of fire, at least until we find Viktor."

"Should I tell her about him?"

"Not yet. If she finds out, she's gonna go after those bastards, and that's exactly what they want. But..."

"What? There's *more*?"

"Yeah. Something you need to know. The Cinques aren't the ones behind all of this. They're pissed at Viktor for trying to take over their piece of the drug trafficking business and us for working with him, but they're not the ones who put the hit on the Ivanovs. They're just the cover. They carried it out but didn't order it."

"Jesus Christ, Nico! How long have you known this? You guys had me out in California for two goddamn years trying to get into the Cinque organization to find out who pulled the trigger on the Ivanovs. And now you're telling me it wasn't the Cinques?"

"No, I'm not saying that. You got the names of the guys who killed the Ivanovs, but the Cinques weren't the ones behind it."

I try to keep my voice steady even though I want to scream my damn head off. "Then who the fuck is after Viktor and Kat?" I say through gritted teeth, my fingers tight around my phone.

"A guy named Remy Valkamir."

"Who is Remy Valkamir?" I hiss. "I've never even heard that name! What the hell does he have to do with this? And why didn't anyone in the Cinque family ever mention him?" Nico always pulls this. He always holds things back until he decides it's time to share. And even now, I'll bet there's a whole lot more he's still holding onto.

Nico is silent for a few seconds while my blood boils. My pulse throbs against my neck, and I struggle to keep my fist from slamming through a wall right now. "Nico, tell me what the you know about this guy. What does he have to do with Viktor's family?"

Nico sighs. "This is for your ears only, Rocco. I'm serious."

"Fine!" I pound the granite countertop. "Tell me what you know about Remy Valkamir!"

"Years ago, when Viktor got started—"

"Remy?" A strangled sound comes from behind me, and I jump off the bar stool, my phone clattering on the counter next to me.

"Kat..." My voice trails off, throat dry. Why the fuck didn't I take this call in the office? How stupid am I?

"Why are you talking about Remy Valkamir?" she shouts, her fists clenched at her sides. "What the hell are you talking about?" She stomps toward me, her cheeks bright red, lips stretched into a tight line. "Answer me!"

I hold up my hands almost on instinct, hoping she gets the message and stands down. Although judging by the murderous look in her eyes, I don't think she's paying much attention to my gestures. In fact, if we're on the topic of hands, I'm pretty sure hers are close to being wrapped around my neck.

And if they find their way there, no way is she letting go.

"How long were you standing there?" I finally ask.

"Long enough to know you're a motherfucking liar!" She lunges for me and shoves me backward. I stumble into the barstool and the wrought iron crashes against the floor tile. The force leaves a long, deep crack along the shiny ceramic surface.

I guess it's a good thing she didn't try to hurl the stool at my head instead.

I try to sideswipe the downed stool, but she keeps coming and my foot gets caught in one of the grooves. I twist around before I fall against the counter and slam my hip into the corner. "Ahh!" I yell, clutching my side.

"You fucking deserve that, you asshole!" She shoves me again, pounding on my chest with her fists. "What about Remy? Why do you even know his name?"

I wince, the sharp pain in my side slicing through me when I turn toward her. "Just stop, okay?"

"Don't you tell me to stop! Don't you ever fucking tell me what to do!" Tears are streaming down her face and her breaths are short and sharp. She looks damn close to hyperventilating, not that it does a thing to her killer instincts. Right now, I can't be sure she wouldn't slice my throat in a hot second if there was a knife in reach. She launches a fist at my jaw, and I swing around to avoid it.

Without a split second to spare.

I grab her wrist and pull her to me. "Kat, I don't know anything about Remy. I swear."

"Liar!" she bellows, grabbing a glass from the counter and hurling it against a wall. It shatters in a million pieces next to the floor crack. "Do you see that? It's my fucking heart! You just broke my heart, you sonofabitch! I trusted you! I opened up to you! And all along, you knew! You knew everything! I heard it all, so don't deny it!"

"Kat, please." I cringe as she picks up a plate and throws it against another wall. "You have to believe me. I don't know anything about Remy."

"And what about the rest?" she hisses. "What about that, Rocco? Don't lie to me again. I heard plenty. You know my mom and sister were killed. You knew it before I told you last night. And you pretended you had no idea." She reaches for the knife block, her hand trembling over the handles. Suddenly, I'm staring at a shiny steel blade.

Fuck, this is how it ends? *Really?*

"How did you know?" she growls, holding the knife up to her cheek.

"Because Nico's family sent me out to California a few years ago to find out who killed them."

"Keep going." She narrows her eyes at me and edges closer. "Don't you even think about lying to me again."

"Look. I didn't know you. They sent me out there because they needed some kind of leverage for your father. They wanted to work with him, knew the history with your mom and sister, and figured if they could get him information he needed, they'd gain his trust. His businesses were suffering, and he needed their money. The Salesis needed his drug connections. It was a win-win."

Kat steps closer. "My father told me it was a random robbery that got out of control."

"It wasn't."

"I never believed him..." Her voice trails off and she rubs her temple with her free hand, the one that isn't ready to lance me with a butcher knife.

"So you know who killed them?" Her voice no longer has the murderous edge to it. Now it just sounds sad. Lost. Alone.

"Yeah." Somehow, I manage to force out the word even though there's a lump the size of a grapefruit lodged in my throat.

"Why would someone kill them?" The knife clatters to the floor, and Kat sinks down next to it. "Why did it happen? And how could he have kept it from me all of this time? I always knew deep down it was bullshit, that it was more than what he told me. And I lived with the guilt of being left behind since that day. He could have told me." She looks at me, her teeth clenched. "You could have told me!"

"I wanted to. I hated lying to you, Kat. But I couldn't go against my orders. And now my ass is a target. The Cinques want me dead for infiltrating their organization and getting that information. That's why my family is going to Florida. We needed to get them out of here." I take a deep breath. "I needed to protect you, too. That was my other order."

"You still haven't told me about Remy."

"I don't know anything about him. This is the first time—"

"He was my boyfriend." Kat's voice is low. Menacing. Angry. "He dropped us off right before...right before..." She pauses. "Did he have something to do with it? Is that what you found out?"

I step toward her, still not sure whether or not she's on the brink of murder in the first degree. "I didn't get to find out. Nico was about to tell me when you came in here. I honestly don't know anything about him."

She looks at me, her lips quivering. I want to wrap my arms around her so badly, but I'm afraid she might pick up the knife and slice my jugular.

A second passes, and I close the distance between us.

I don't give a shit anymore.

She lets me hold her, even though her body stiffens against me. I wait for her to say something, to do something, to curse me some more, to scream, hit, anything. When she finally speaks, the words slice into my insides deeper than any knife gash ever could. "You told me you'd never let anything hurt me, that you'd keep me safe." She scoffs, pushing me away. "Well, you just killed me, Rocco. Tore my heart out of my chest and shredded it." A sob escapes her chest. "You wanted it, and now you have it. In a million fucking pieces!"

## Chapter Seventeen
# KATARINA

I run out of the kitchen without another glance at Rocco. I can't look. I'm too damn close to crumbling, and I need to get out of here.

"Kat, please!"

I don't answer him. I grab my coat and pull it on over my sweats, my heart thumping so hard that it deafens me. I came back into the kitchen to see if he had another bar of soap since my search had come up empty.

Thank God I did.

I found out that he's as much of a liar as everyone else around me.

I knew it wasn't drug addicts looking for cash.

I knew it wasn't just a coincidence!

Goddamn them all! And goddamn my father most of all. He's the reason they're dead. He did this to our family!

The tears are so close, but I have to get the hell out of here. I need to know what the fuck is going on, once and for all. I throw my cell phone into my bag and stop only to take a deep breath. Stoli 2 rests his head at my feet, no doubt sensing my not-so-hidden rage, and I rub his ears. "I'm sorry, boy. I wanted to stay with you, but I have to leave. I'm so sorry," I whisper, jumping to my feet.

Rocco's keys are on a table in the foyer. I grab them and push past him where he's standing in his sweatpants. "What the hell are you doing with my keys?"

"I'm stealing your car," I say, pulling open the front door and walking outside into the cool, crisp air.

"The fuck you are!" He runs after me, barefoot and shirtless. His fingers close around my wrist, and he yanks me backward with a small amount of force. I twirl around and launch a crushing blow to the side of his face. "Don't you dare touch me! You'll never touch me again!"

He stands there, his mouth hanging open, and my pulse rockets. "You wanna try me? Next time I won't be so gentle, you asshole!"

I stomp toward his car, feeling his eyes burn a hole into my back. I open the door of his prized Maserati, get in, and slam the door shut before gunning the motor. I put the car in gear and press my foot on the gas. The tires squeal on the pavement as I fly out of the driveway. The scent of burning rubber makes me smile. "Take that, prick. I'm gonna run this bitch into the ground."

I glance over at him before I peel down the street, and that's when the tears decide to spill over, blurring my vision.

Unfortunately, it wasn't in enough time for me to miss the look of anguish on his face as he hangs onto Stoli 2's collar to keep him from running after me.

I downshift and the sports car screeches to a halt a couple of blocks away. My fingers are trembling, and my vision is fuzzy with the damn tears that seem to have become a part of my daily routine. Looks like Kat the badass decided to morph into Kat the basket case.

Yet again.

I don't know how to deal with this tearful bitch.

My pulse throbs, thumping against my neck as I stab some

numbers into my phone and let it ring. And ring. And...nothing. Not even voicemail.

Papa's not picking up. Where the hell is he? Is he still in mourning, for fuck's sake? Is he sorry for all of the lies he's told me for the past eight years? Or for fucking up so many of our family's businesses that our money is dwindling more and more by the day? Is he sorry for ruining my life? For ending the lives of Mom and Lili?

These questions pop through my mind like bullets ricocheting off a cement wall. I slam my phone against the steering wheel before dialing Alexi. Maybe he's heard from Papa.

"Goddamit, Kat! Where the hell have you been?" he shouts into the phone as soon as the line connects. "You're supposed to be with me! You never listen. Instead, you go to the animal shelter without telling me and then disappear from there. I left texts and voicemails all day and all night! I thought you'd been taken!"

"Alexi, just tell me where I can find my father," I say, trying to keep my voice even. It registers that he knew I was at the shelter, but that's not a shock. If he was looking for me, he'd have found my car. Based on what little I heard of Rocco's one-sided conversation, it's pretty clear why Alexi was so pissed off at me for running off without telling him. Papa has made his bed and mine, and he obviously fucked with the wrong people this time.

But screw that. If these people...my heart clenches...if *Remy* had anything to do with Mom and Lili dying, let them come after me. For eight years, I've wanted to find who did this to my family and make them suffer. And now that I'm so close, I can almost taste the revenge on my tongue.

I don't need anyone to protect me. Not Alexi. Not Rocco. Not Papa.

"He's in a meeting," Alexi says, a harsh edge to his voice. "He came back to town this morning and went right to Red Square. But he cannot be disturbed."

"Screw that!" I shriek.

"Kat, don't go there alone! At least let me come with you."

"I don't need a fucking babysitter!" I yell, pounding on the steering wheel with my fist.

"Look, whatever is happening there isn't something he wanted you to see. So just calm the fuck down and pick me up."

A gasp escapes my lips. Holy shit. What if I wasn't seeing things that night at Max's club? What if it really was Remy?

I take a few deep breaths, not that it does much good. Rage bubbles deep inside of me, so damn close to erupting with a force even I can't imagine.

"I know you're thinking about it," Alexi says. "Just take a breath and come over. I'll be waiting."

I end the call and throw my phone on the seat next to me. I fist my hands and clutch the sides of my head, letting out the most horrifying scream in this quiet New Jersey suburb. Much as I hate to admit it, Alexi is right. I don't know what this meeting is about or who it's with, and I don't ever go into Red Square unprotected. You just never know. And stupid me, I didn't think before I stormed out of Rocco's house.

Seems like that's happening to me a lot more lately. That shit stops *now*.

I lean down and feel around on the floor under both seats until my finger hits something hard.

Bingo.

I slide out a gun case and unzip it to reveal a gleaming black Beretta. I pick it up and turn it over in my hands. Fully loaded. Fucking fabulous.

The tears have long since dried up, and I can feel the badass seeping back into my veins.

It feels good. I've missed it. And now I'm ready to unleash it.

*Thank you, Rocco.*

I put the car into gear and shift up, merging back onto the road. I clutch the steering wheel, pressing my foot on the gas. I manage to ignore all of the questions flooding my mind as I drive to Alexi's apartment.

My phone dances on the seat next to me, buzzing with intensity. Someone is trying really hard to get to me. Alexi, Rocco, who the fuck ever. I never take my eyes off the road. Whoever is calling me can just wait like I have for the past eight years!

But today the wait is finally over. I don't know who or what I'll find at Red Square, but I won't leave until I get the answers I need to hear, the ones I should have heard a very long time ago.

Papa kept me in the dark for too long.

Today, I will make things right...bring every seedy word of truth into the light...one way or another.

## Chapter Eighteen
# ROCCO

Nico's car barely screeches to a halt before I pull open the door and jump inside. "Okay, where the hell are we going?"

"I still can't believe you let her steal your damn car," Nico grumbles.

"It's not stealing if I watch her drive away and don't try to stop her." I rake a hand through my hair.

Nico glares at me out of the corner of his eye. "This is a goddamn mess. Get Max on the phone."

I stab Max's phone number into my phone. This feels like déjà vu. We've been here before.

So many fucking times before.

This time, my ass is in the hot seat and Kat's ass...I can't even think about that right now.

"Have you tried calling Kat?"

I nod. "Nonstop. No answer." Max's voice comes on the line. "What's up, douchebag? I'm in the middle of—"

"Max, I need your help."

"Christ, I love those words," he mutters. "Means someone's getting fucked up. *Bad*. Tell me when and where. I'll be there shaking my fucking bells."

"Go to my parents' house. I was supposed to drive them to the airport, but shit has gone sideways with the Cinques. I need you to stay with them."

"You need me to *babysit*? Where the hell are you?"

"I'm with Nico. Viktor is gone, and Kat..." I let out a frustrated sigh. "She took off, probably went after him."

"Why are you keeping tabs on the Ivanovs?"

"Put him on speaker," Nico grunts, pressing on the gas and merging onto the New Jersey Turnpike.

I hit the button. "Okay."

"Max, there's a lot of shit happening right now. Rocco and I are heading into the city. I was supposed to meet Viktor today at Red Square, but the guy has fallen off the face of the Earth. It's not like him to disappear like that. And Kat heard some things today that she shouldn't have because Rocco opened his big fucking mouth."

"I thought she was in the shower," I mumble.

"Whoa, hey, she was at your place? In *your* shower? And you weren't in there with her? Dude, what the hell is wrong with you?" Max lets out a loud chuckle, and I roll my eyes. Fucking asshole.

"Just go to my parents' house. Tell them to reschedule their flight and that I'll call when I can. I don't have time to sit on the phone and answer any questions right now. My dad will know to lay low."

"Did the Cinques grab Viktor?" Max asks.

The car is silent for a minute. "I don't know," Nico says. "But somebody did, that's for shit sure. And this asshole next to me will be next if we don't exterminate them first."

"Okay," Max says. "I'll take care of it."

I click off the phone. "Nico, tell me the deal with Remy Valkamir. Kat went fucking nuts when she heard his name. Said they dated back when...you know."

Nico taps his fingertips on the steering wheel and swerves around a car before heading into the Holland Tunnel. He takes a deep breath and lets it out slowly before finally speaking. "When Viktor first started growing his business in the United States, he made a lot of enemies. He killed people to get what he wanted. One of the men had been a longtime business rival. Viktor took over his territory and killed him. Remy is the guy's son. The mom had been pregnant with him and was sent back to Russia. She was killed, too. Somehow, he found his way back here and has been plotting ever since. He's the one who ordered the hit on Viktor's family. He got in close. Knew Viktor's schedule. Was Kat's boyfriend. He's the reason she's still alive. He kept her alive as leverage. After the hit, Viktor was warned to pull back from all of his businesses and let the Cinques take over. Kat would live. Remy would watch Viktor's empire crumble after his life had been shattered. Just like what he and his mother had to face. That's why Viktor came to us. He knew they'd end up taking everything and needed our backing to keep himself operational."

I rub the sides of my head. "It doesn't make sense. Why is this happening now? It's been eight years."

"Kat killing Raines was the final straw. Our association with Viktor put us on the hit list for the Cinques. Then you did your own brand of damage when you were out in California, so I don't have to tell you why there's a target on *your* ass."

"Yeah, I'm clear on that, thanks."

"Ian Raines had fucked Viktor over left and right, and Viktor let it go because he knew that going after Raines would get Kat killed. Raines was a big money maker for the Cinques, and he was slowly crushing Viktor's businesses. When Kat got wind of what Raines was doing, how he was stealing from Viktor and how Viktor was allowing it to happen, she took matters into her own hands. Killing Raines cost the Cinques a ton of cash. And now the Cinques want to take back what's theirs and collect on the debt."

"So why not just kill Viktor? Why does Kat have anything to do with this?

"Remy wants Viktor to suffer the way he and his mom did.

That's why they killed his wife and daughter. Killing Viktor would put him out of his misery. Too easy." He pauses and looks at me. "They're gonna kill Kat and make him see how bad life can get when you lose everything. Remy doesn't give a shit about money. He only wants revenge."

My throat tightens, but I still manage to choke out some words. "Do you really th—?"

"It's what I'd do," he says, his voice sharp and cold, void of any emotion.

"Jesus Christ," I moan, dialing Kat's number once again. Still nothing. "Do you think she's there? Is that why Viktor wanted you to meet him at Red Square? He was trying to get you down there so the Cinques would take care of you at—?"

"I don't know, okay?" Nico slams his foot on the brake and turns to face me, his face red. "I don't have the answers, Rocco. I get that you're nervous about Kat. That's why we're here. We're gonna find her."

I cover my face with my hands. "Fuck! I shoulda told Max to come here instead of going to my parents' house. We need his brand of crazy right now, and one of the other guys coulda watched the house."

"Do you think I'm an idiot?" Nico accelerates as the light turns green and hangs a right down a darkened side street in lower Manhattan. "Why do you and Max constantly question me? Have I really ever steered you wrong? Fucking ever?"

"I know, I know!" I slam my fist on the door. "This is just really bad."

"No shit, Sherlock!" He pulls into an alleyway and stops the car behind a large dumpster. "Come on. Red Square is around the corner and they'll be watching. The car'll be fine here, and we'll get in through the back entrance."

"Are you sure we don't need backup?"

"Do I need to ask my question again?"

"No..." I feel around under my coat. "Fuck me, I don't have a gun."

Nico rolls his eyes and reaches under the seat behind him. He pulls out three guns, keeping two for himself.

"How come you get two?"

"Because you're the moron who let Kat steal your car *and* your gun." He nods at the door. "Let's move."

This area of the city is usually pretty dead, today being no exception. And I'm sure that's what the Cinques were counting on, too.

Lucky them.

Unlucky for the rest of us.

We run across the street and creep through another alleyway behind a dilapidated factory until we reach the fenced-in clearing behind Red Square.

"I think this is a stupid idea. We need backup," I mutter, unlocking the safety and peering around us.

"Relax. We'll be ready in one, two, three—"

My phone vibrates in my pocket and I put my hand on Nico's arm. "Wait," I whisper. I stare at the phone. It's a text from Max.

*Lindy's missing. Your dad said she went out this morning to pick up some things for the trip. Never came back.*

My heart jumps into my throat and damn-near chokes me as I hold out the phone. Nico backs away from the door. "Sonofabitch," he growls, looking at his watch.

Gio and Sammy, two of his security guys from his nightclub, run through a hole in one of the fences. Nico cocks an eyebrow at me but says nothing.

"Nico," I hiss. "What the fuck is going on? We need to find Lindy! Jesus Christ, if they took her...if they lay a finger on her..." I fist my hair and pace around, trying to think. She disappeared this morning. Kat took off this morning. Nico was supposed to meet Viktor this morning.

The Cinques want us all dead and they'll use whomever they need to get to us.

Including my sister, who, up until this point, thought I was a bouncer at a nightclub.

My phone buzzes again, and Lindy's name flashes on the screen.

Relief floods my body, and I let out a deep breath I didn't even realize I'd been holding. I stab the Accept button.

"Lindy! Where the fuck—?"

"Hold that thought for just a second, Lucchese."

My gut twists as the low voice on the other end of the line hisses into my ear. I know that voice. I've had nightmares about hearing it again.

But I always knew it would happen. I knew I'd never be able to hide forever.

"Where the hell is my sister?" I growl into the phone, my hand shaking.

"Don't panic. Yet. She's in good hands. Although, if you and Salesi don't show up soon, I can't promise that things won't go in a very bad direction for her."

An icy sensation weaves around my heart and squeezes tight, so tight the sensation makes me yelp. "Don't you dare lay a fucking finger on her!"

"You're in no position to make demands. We'll be waiting."

*Click.*

My skull throbs, and I clutch the sides of my head. "They took her. They took Lindy. Fuck, we need to get her back. We need to get them both back!" I whisper-shout.

"Calm the fuck down!" Nico puts his hands on my shoulders. "Pull your shit together before we go in there, Rocco. I need your head straight, you got it?"

I nod, rubbing the back of my neck. Tiny beads of sweat pebble om my skin even though it's freezing outside. I swallow hard and look at Sammy and Gio. My stomach rolls, and I'm pretty sure whatever I shoveled into my mouth for breakfast is about to make a re-appearance.

A shudder runs through me as Nico grabs the handle and pulls open the door. He creeps inside, crouching low, gun drawn. A shadow crosses in front of me, and I don't even have time to think before swinging my arm out and bludgeoning the bastard with my own piece. A loud thud rattles the floor as the faceless guy hits the floor. Nico nods at Gio and Sammy.

Okay. They're here. And they're clearly waiting.

Blood rushes between my ears as I follow Nico through a doorway. I'm covering his back, hoping that Gio and Sammy have mine. Another loud thud makes me jump and Sammy shrugs, standing over another beefy guy who is face-down on the floor. I give him the thumbs-up, turning back to Nico. He holds out his hand and a tearful voice makes my skin crawl.

At this point, I have no idea how many guys they have in there. I don't know if Viktor is alive or dead. I don't know anything.

"Fuck this shit," I mutter, pointing my gun toward the ceiling and firing a shot.

Nico throws me backward into a wall. "Are you crazy?"

"We need them to bring the fight here. This place is a maze! They'll take us out one by one if we try to get inside. You've been here! You know how many hidden rooms there are. This way, they know we're here and we'll be ready for them. I'm going in."

Nico shakes his head and twists backward against the wall next to me. "Christ Almighty, are you seriously that fucked in the head?"

"Yep. I need to create a distraction, otherwise we're all gonna get plugged. I have to find the girls. If they're here, it's because they're waiting for *us*." I look in every direction before tearing out of our hiding spot. "Cover me."

"You're insane."

I shrug. "Not really. Just finally ready to face this shit and end it already." I clap him on the shoulder and crouch around a wall before jogging down a short hallway leading into the underbelly of the Russian bratva.

I'm the reason why Lindy is here in the first place. And Kat? Her being here is on me, too. I let her go. I watched her leave.

I peek around a doorway and a shot ricochets off the wall next to me. "Fuck!" I yelp, creeping around a corner and firing off a few quick shots behind me until I make it to the next room. It's dark, save for the bit of light coming from I guess what must be the bar area. I hear angry footsteps and some arguing in Russian. Deep, male voices.

A faint moan makes me jerk sideways, and I almost lose my footing. I feel my way up the wall, praying there's a light switch. My fingers hit something small and hard, and I flip it upward before taking cover behind what feels like a table leg. "Viktor?" I whisper, taking a few steps toward him.

Behind me, all hell is breaking loose, but in here, it's silent.

Deadly silent.

His body is crumpled in a chair, his face bloody and bruised. His dark hair sticks up in a million different directions, and his usual Armani is torn and tattered. The guy looks like he's been to hell and back — ten times over.

Beaten to shit.

I never thought I'd see the day.

His head rolls backward, his eyes open a slit because they're so swollen and cut. His breathing is labored, and body slack in the chair. I stare, because it's hard not to gape at this bad ass, Russian mob boss, broken beyond repair. Given my own experiences, I can honestly understand why people would want to do this to him. The guy is a complete prick — evil, malicious, and lethal as a shot between the eyes.

Hell, I'd have liked to take a crack at him myself, especially after hearing what Kat had gone through for all of those years.

What she continues to go through now.

But there isn't time to unpack any of that. I need to find Kat and Lindy. Then I need to get them the hell out of here before anyone gets hurt.

If that hasn't already happened.

I inch closer to Viktor and kneel down next to him, loosening the ropes binding his wrists and feet. Heavy footsteps get louder and then another round of gunfire explodes around me. "Fuck!" I grunt. "Viktor, where is Kat?"

"Alexi...supposed to be watching...can't find her..." His weak voice trails off, eyes drooping closed.

I shake him, my voice rising in panic. "She's not here? Where is she? Who is she with?"

Another low groan rumbles deep in his throat. "...Remy...has her..." A thick cough erupts from his heaving chest.

"Remy is here?"

But Viktor doesn't answer. He's in and out of consciousness, which means we may have a little time. If Nico is right, if they really want him to witness Kat's murder as their final play, they'd need to keep him alive. And awake.

Maybe she's not here.

Maybe she escaped.

Maybe—

I can't sit here any longer, wondering what the hell *may* have happened.

I have to act. Now. Diversion or not.

I need to find my girls.

I creep toward the doorway and push it open. The hallway is clear.

Quiet.

The aftermath?

I don't have time to check on the guys. I just have to pray most of those gunshots took out the enemy.

I stay low to the ground as I inch forward down the hall. The stench of stale beer and cigarettes makes my stomach roil. I swallow hard, but my throat is so damn tight. Feels like an invisible hand is choking me.

Something tells me that before I make it out of this dump, there will be a real hand reaching around my neck and squeezing.

A loud shriek pierces the air and I jump. Fuck, that's Lindy...

I don't think. I don't wait. I don't breathe.

I just run in the direction of the cry. "Lindy!" I yell, kicking open another door. Two guys are sitting at a table, snorting lines of something. One of them leaps up from his seat and goes to grab his gun...

Two seconds too late. I fire off a few shots until they both hit the floor. "Lindy!" I yell again.

The whimpering gets louder, and I know I'm close. The only problem is, so does everyone else.

I dart down another hallway. It seems like this turn is taking me deeper into the Russian den of sin, and the farther in I go, the less likely I will be to get out. They'll corner me from behind, and I know someone...or a bunch of someones...is waiting for me to come pounding down doors.

More gunshots make my breath hitch. I stop and slam back into a wall outside another room, trying to pull in some air so I don't suffocate before I've had a chance to end this nightmare. This is the one. The cries for help are deafening. Someone is yelling something in Russian. Footsteps pound on the floor behind me. I'm cornered. I've got two choices. Storm the room and take out whomever I can in the process or wait here like a sitting duck.

I don't like either option.

I arch my back, lifting my leg to kick open the door, ignoring all of the warnings bleeping in my brain. As far as I know, my backup is toast. I don't know who's coming for me, and I don't know what waits for me behind this door.

All I know is I have to make a move while I still can.

With a final deep breath, I launch my leg out at the same time a large body hurls itself at me, pummeling me to the dirty, cigarette butt-covered floor.

"You go in there, you're dead, asshole," Nico mutters. "Use your brain, dammit!"

I twist my head around to find Nico panting over me. The front of his coat is splattered with dark red spots and he grimaces as he pops another clip into his gun.

"Fuck, man. Are you hit?"

"Just grazed my arm. I'm fine. That's more than I can say for Gio," he says through clenched teeth.

"What about Sammy?"

"He's okay. Took out about four of these assholes and now he's trying to find Xiomar Cinque. I know he's here. Those were his guys we took out, not the Russians."

"And I found Vik—"

Nico nods before I can even finish. "I know. I saw." He lifts an eyebrow. "Are you ready for this?"

"No, but we're going in anyway." I leap to my feet, and Nico follows. "Okay, on three. One, two—"

"Three, motherfuckers!"

I jump back as Max launches himself at the closed door, kicking it open and landing feet first inside. With guns in each hand, he starts shooting. "It's a fucking party now, assholes!"

My eyes dart left and right as gunfire blares out in the large space. Bodies hit the ground as Max and Nico take them out one by one. Shots are being fired in every direction, but where are the girls? I know I heard Lindy from outside the door. And Cinque…what the hell did he—?

I pop a couple of shots at two guys who look like they've had two bottles too many of vodka, and they collapse onto the floor. But there's a small army headed in here now. I can hear the shouting and the gunfire behind the walls. The A-team is about to attack.

Max and Nico dive behind a metal table and flip it onto its side as bullets pepper the top of it. Max peeks his head around the side, still shooting. "Rocco, go and find the girls!"

I turn on my heel, my legs twitching to run through the place. I leave Nico and Max, and head in the opposite direction. They're here. I know they are. I creep toward another doorway, away from the firefight and stumble into a wall. "Fuck!" I groan, collapsing to the floor next to Gio's limp and bloody body. Dammit, Gio was a good guy. How much more blood is gonna be on my hands at the end of this shit show? I say a silent prayer that Max and Nico can hold off the rest of the guys, and that Sammy doesn't get his ass shot up before he can get there to help them. I pull myself off the floor and limp around a corner. There's only one more room…only one more chance…

I grip the handle and push open the door.

"Mnph!" A muffled cry makes my breath hitch. "Lindy!" I whisper. "Thank fuck!"

She stomps her feet, her eyes wild. "Achahhhuut!" Her cries are muffled, and I can't make out what the hell she's trying to say.

I hold up a hand, the gun cocked and ready in my other one, just in case. "Shh, it's okay. I'll get you—"

A strong hand yanks me backward, a heavy metal piece pressed hard against my temple. Goddammit. I never bothered to look behind me…

"Were you looking for me, Lucchese?" A deep voice hisses into my ear. "Because I've been looking for *you*."

Xiomar Cinque's grip on the back of my coat tightens. "So has your sister. Pretty girl. I could have some real fun with her. Tell me, did you ever think about Lindy when you were infiltrating my organization? Did you ever think about your parents? Your grandmother? Did you ever really think you were gonna get away with this shit and not suffer the consequences?"

I clench my teeth. *Please, please, please no…* "Xiomar, you have me, okay? Just leave everyone else out of this. I'm the one you want. Forget the rest of them."

He lets out a dry laugh. "I'm a greedy sonofabitch, what can I say?"

Lindy's whimpers are muffled by the duct tape slapped over her mouth. Anger bubbles in my veins. "Let her go, you bastard."

Xiomar fists the back of my hair and pulls my head back so his mouth is practically against my ear. "I want to make sure you hear this, Rocco. You're not exactly in a position to be making requests. You got that? You fucked with me, with my family, and with my business. There's no way in hell you walk outta here today. No," he growls through clenched teeth. "The only way you leave here is in a body bag. And that's when I'm gonna go to work on you."

I swallow hard. If he wanted me dead, I'd be face down in a ditch right now. My spine stiffens as he yanks me out of the room. "Don't worry. She'll be fine. For the time being, anyway. We have some business to handle and then you'll get to watch what I do next. I want you to have a front seat for it."

Tears stream down Lindy's face and she lets out a scream as Xiomar pushes me into the hallway and shoves me forward against a wall. "Don't worry. You can say goodbye later."

I catch a glimpse of a dark shadow moving slowly around the corner. A hail of gunshots rings out, pelting the walls around us. I dive to the ground, my fingertips closing on my own gun. Xiomar crouches on the ground, arm straight out, firing off a round. Or ten. I don't know. I lose track. I crawl around him and run back into the room where Lindy struggles to get loose from the zip ties digging into her wrists. "Stop," I say, grabbing my Swiss Army knife from my pocket. I pull off the duct tape from her mouth and she lets out a shriek that can shatter glass. Her teeth chatter as panicked words tumble from her lips. "Rocco, what the fuck is going on? Who are these people? What do they want? They grabbed me this morning when I went for last minute things at the drug store. There was an SUV, and a guy who had his arm in a sling...and he needed help, so I stopped. And then he pulled me inside! And I saw guns! And he said your name. And Nico's. And—"

I take her by the shoulder and give her a gentle shake. "Listen, I know you're scared. I am, too. There's a lot you don't know, and right now, I just don't have time to explain. Just tell me one thing." I look straight into her eyes. "Have you seen Kat at all?"

"No," she whispers, swiping at the tears streaming down her cheeks. "Why would she be here?"

I shake my head. "Not now. Right now, I need to get you out

of here. We're gonna go back out there, and I'm gonna get you to the exit. And then—"

"The fuck you are!" I jump at Nico's voice behind me. "Where the hell is Xiomar?"

I rub the back of my neck and squint toward the ceiling. Sonofabitch. "He's not out there? He didn't get hit?"

"No, shithead." Nico groans. "You let him get away? You didn't shoot him in the fucking head when you had the chance?"

"My sister was tied up in the next room." I roll my eyes. "Sorry I wasn't thinking."

"Look, we need to get the hell out of here now. It's only a matter of time before they come for us. Where are Max and Sammy?"

"I left them to come find you." Nico shakes his head. "I don't like this, though. Something doesn't seem right. And where the fuck is Kat?"

"I don't know." I nod to Nico. "But you need to get Lindy out of here. I'm not leaving until I find Kat."

"You don't even know if she's here. Your car isn't anywhere around." Nico pops his head out into the hallway. "Okay, we're clear. Let's go." He inches toward the exit, breaking into a full run as we get closer to the door. "Maybe Max will—"

*Pop! Crack! Pop!*

Shit.

Where the hell *is* Max, anyway?

A shiver slithers over my skin. "Get Lindy out of here. I'm going back in. Max and Kat are still in there. I'm not leaving without them."

"I'm not leaving you alone," Nico grunts. "It's suicide."

"I can handle it. He saved my ass. It's my turn to repay the debt. Please, just get Lindy out. You know you can't stay. You've got the family to run."

*Bang! Crack! Pop!*

"You took a bullet for me," Nico growls. "I'm not letting you go back in there."

I lace my fingers with Lindy's and squeeze. "Nico is gonna get you out—"

*Pop! Pop! Pop!*

I clap a hand over Lindy's mouth just before a loud scream escapes. "Shh," I whisper. "It's gonna be okay."

Heavy footsteps thump toward us, and I push Lindy behind me, pressing her against the wall. Nico crouches low, his gun pointed in the direction of the sound.

"Are you guys thinking about bailing on me and Sammy?" Max lumbers over, a crooked grin on his face. "What a bunch of pussies. Good thing I showed up when I did. You guys would be six feet under by now without me coming in to save the day." He gives me a punch in the shoulder. "Tell me something. Where the hell are all of the big guys? Vik is still tied to that chair, half dead. Everyone else is either dead or gone."

"Or that's what they want us to think," I mutter.

"It doesn't make sense, but we need to get Viktor out of here." Nico runs a hand through his hair and looks at me. "Are you sure Kat came here?"

"No, I have no idea where she went. But I'm sure she went looking for Viktor and he's here, so where else would she go?"

Nico's eyes drop to the floor, letting out a deep sigh. He's not saying it, but I know what he's thinking. They've already got her, and that's why Viktor is here. They beat the shit out of him and they're going to make him watch them kill the last of his family. "Xiomar didn't kill you."

"Wow, you're fucking observant," I say, kicking a stone on the ground. "No, he didn't. And I didn't kill him. So where the hell did he go? And why didn't he take me out?"

Nico fists his hair. "I don't know, okay?"

"You're supposed to know everything, though," Max says, waggling his eyebrows. "You never share any of it, but you know it all."

Nico grabs Max by the collar. "Shut the hell up," he growls.

"Why do these people want to kill you?" Lindy sniffles. "Why is this happening? Oh my God, I don't want to die! I don't want any of us to die! Rocco, we have to leave and go to the police. They'll help us, right?"

I exchange a look with Max and Nico. "Uh, no, actually. They won't. We, um, we play for different teams, us and the cops."

Lindy's eyes can't possibly get any bigger in this second. "Let's just pray I have a chance to explain all of this later." I nod at Nico. "In the meantime, get her out of here. Put her in your car and get her the hell out of the city."

"I'm not leaving without you" Lindy cries, throwing her arms around my neck. "Don't make me go alone. I'm so scared!"

"What the fuck is going on over here? You guys having a private party out here while I plug these cocksuckers?" Sammy jogs over and peeks over his shoulder. "I think I got 'em all."

Max pokes him. "Dickhead. You got like three of them. Don't try to steal all the credit."

Sammy grins and nods at Lindy. "Why's she still here? You idiots want her to get killed?"

Nico grabs Sammy's collar and pushes him out the door. "I'm gonna walk you through the back lot to make sure it's clear." He drops his keys into Sammy's hand. "Get her out of the city as fast as you can and take her back to Rocco's parents' house. The guys are there watching over things. We'll get Viktor out of here and figure out what to do next."

Sammy nods and clasps Lindy's hand. "Come on. Don't worry, we'll be fine."

Lindy's face makes her doubts about that pretty clear. She turns a tearful eye at me, her lips curling into a small smile. "I love you," she whispers before hugging me one last time. "Please be careful."

"I'll see you at home soon." I ruffle her hair.

"Promise?" she asks.

I nod, poking Sammy. "Go. Now."

They creep out the back door, and I turn to Max. "What the hell is going on here?"

He shakes his head. "I don't know, man. Nobody tells me shit." He pops a new clip into his gun. "But we need to get Vik outta here pronto. If any of those shitheads are still standing, they're gonna be back soon."

Those words ring out in my head. Xiomar could have taken me out but didn't. He disappeared instead, leaving us here to fight off his guys. Leaving Viktor.

*Why?*

An icy hand snakes around my heart and squeezes. "They're coming back," I croak. "Viktor is here waiting. They didn't kill him because they want him alive to see them..." I swallow hard. "To see them kill Kat."

"That doesn't explain why Xiomar didn't kill you when he had the chance."

A loud clicking sound from behind me makes me stumble forward into Max.

"So smart, yet so fucking stupid." I put my hand on the wall to regain my footing and twist around to see Xiomar grinning and shaking his head. "The same reason why I brought your pretty little sister down here. You're gonna watch me kill *her* before I put a bullet in your pea-sized brain."

## Chapter Nineteen
# KATARINA

"How long have you known about this meeting?" I take a sharp turn, swerving Rocco's car around a narrow corner behind Red Square. "Why didn't you tell me about it?"

"I thought you knew," Alexi says. "Besides, you've been disappearing every fucking day, Katarina. He told you to stay close, that these assholes Raines worked with are getting close. But no, you always do what you want to do. You never listen!"

"Look, I can take care of myself! I've told you before that I don't need a babysitter!" The tires screech against the pavement as I pull into the back lot of Red Square. I squint in the sunlight to see a dark-haired figure running toward the back entrance of Red Square. Alone. "Is that Nico?" I slam on the brakes and put the car into Park. "Why is he here? Is he meeting with—?"

I jump out of the car, ready to run over to Nico when someone steps out of one of the black F-150s parked along the perimeter, blocking any view from passers-by. I can't make out the face of the guy, but he's tall and lean. There's something vaguely familiar about the way he carries himself. How weird that I'd even pick up on it. He walks toward Nico, reaching a hand into his jacket.

I watch the scene unfold in slow motion. I try to run, but something pulls me backward. My feet are still kicking up sand and stones, but my body is being held by a set of strong hands. I fight against them, but it's no use.

I can't hear anything...all sounds around me are muted. "Nico! No!" My mouth forms the words, but no sounds escape. I try to scream, but silence consumes me, save for the two shots to the chest that send Nico crumbling to the ground.

"No, no, no!" I shriek, struggling against Alexi's chest. "Let me go! I have to help him!" Tears stream down my face as the ever-present nightmare rears its head once again. "I can't let this happen again! He needs me!" I yank out of Alexi's grip and run toward Nico, pressing my head against his chest to see if I can make out a heartbeat.

I don't look at the man who just shot him.

I don't look back at Alexi.

I just stare at my friend. "Please, God, no."

"Must bring back memories."

A chill slithers around my insides. That voice...I know that voice...

I twist my head around, yelping as Alexi pulls me off the ground by the back of my coat. "Remy?" I whisper.

He grins at me, his dark eyes filled with malice. "That's right, Kat. It's been a long time, and I've thought about you every day." Remy walks toward me, his face twisted into a nasty grimace. "Of the things I'd do to you...the things I'd make your father watch me do to you." He nods at Alexi. "Get her inside."

Alexi shoots out his hand, pointing a gun at my temple. My throat is so tight, I can barely squeeze out a breath. "What the fuck are you doing?"

He narrows his eyes, leaning in close. "For years, I've been a second-class citizen in this family. I've killed for this family, I've made a shit ton of money for this family, and what do I get? Fucking nothing!" An evil grin stretches across his face. "But that changes today. I'm finally gonna get the respect and the money I deserve."

"You sold us out?" I shriek. I launch a fist at his jaw, and he barely stumbles. Bastard! I'm so off my goddamn game right now, and processing all of this is more than I can handle. "Why? My father took care of you! He gave you everything!"

Nico is still sprawled on the ground, blood pooling behind him. My heart aches just thinking of his family and Shaye. I couldn't save him.

Again, I let it happen! I watched and did nothing!

Motherfucker!

Alexi's hand explodes against my cheek with a sharp sting that hurts worse than a hive full of wasps. "No! He gave you everything! He only took from me..." His head nods in Remy's direction. "And my brother."

"Your..." My eyes widen. "...your *brother?*" I manage to rasp out that final word.

Alexi yanks my head back by the hair. "Your father murdered *our* father. He took me in when I was very young to ease his guilt. Told my mother he'd give me a good life here. Then he forced my mother to go back to Russia. She was pregnant with Remy. I never got to know my own brother because of him! My mother was told to stay away from me or else he'd kill me, too. So she did. And I gave my loyalty to the man who ripped apart my family. He used me, day after day, year after year."

"He treated you like his own son!"

Alexi pulls my hair harder, the pain making my eyes water. "I was just leverage to him. He told my mother if she tried to get me back, he'd kill me." He leans closer, his forehead pressed against mine. "And that's exactly what Remy told him when he had your mother and sister killed. Follow *my* rules or I kill Katarina." The disdain in Alexi's voice makes my gut twist. How could I have been so blind to all of this? He was like a brother to me, and all the while, he was plotting to destroy my family the way my father destroyed his. I trusted him, and only him.

"Everyone always played by his rules. And when I was old enough to find out the truth, I decided to make a few of my own rules. He owed me that after taking everything from me. But then he violated the rules by giving you too much power. Now you both die."

The tears flow hard and fast. My stomach rolls, bile rising in my throat, the wounds torn open yet again. "You killed my mother and sister?" I ask Remy. "But you told me...you told me you loved me. I gave you everything," I whisper.

"And why do you think you're the one still living?" Remy asks in a low voice. He nods at Alexi. "Get her inside. It's time."

Alexi drags me away from Nico's cold body, and I claw at the ground to slow him down. "Please don't do this. I can't leave him out here. Alexi, don't—"

He glowers at me. "Your father wouldn't give a shit about leaving him out here. His only concern would be who he can screw next for cash."

"I'm not my father!" I leap up off the ground and hurl myself at Alexi, my fists flying in every which direction. I want to cause him pain, deep, searing, scorching pain, the same type of pain I've lived with, and I dig my fingernails into his throat.

"Get the off me, you crazy bitch," he says, pushing me off of him and shoving me at Remy. "You never did learn to think before you did shit. You're about to learn that lesson now."

Remy closes his hand over my wrist and pushes open the door. He drags me behind him, walking around the bodies sprawled on the concrete floor. Alexi presses a gun into my spine as we walk, and the nightmare continues.

Will I ever fucking wake up?

Is death what finally sets me free from this living hell?

"Viktor!" Remy bellows, his voice echoing in the halls as we walk.

Tears form behind my eyes, and I blink them back. There is no way I'm letting them escape right now. No, I need to keep my shit together right now and figure out how I'm going to get myself and Papa out of this. Alive.

Remy flings open the door to my father's expansive office, and I swallow a sob when I see Papa tied to a chair. It looks like he's been beaten within an inch of his life, but when he sees me, tears pool in his blue eyes...eyes that are normally so cold, they can ice over an ocean in the tropics.

"Papa..." I whisper.

"Yes." Remy leans in close to my ear. "But Viktor isn't the only one who's going to suffer for his sins today." He gently tugs on a strand of my hair, just like he used to do back when...I swallow hard...back when I didn't know he was a psycho with a deadly vendetta against my family. Back when I thought he loved me and wasn't plotting to murder my mother and sister. "See, people always get so fucking greedy. They don't care who they hurt to get what they want. They betray confidences when they've promised loyalty." He shakes his head. "And we don't like that. People who pull that shit need to pay, too." He straightens up. "Xiomar!"

The side door of the office swings open, and I swallow hard when Rocco's dark eyes meet mine.

"Where's the girl?" Remy demands. "You said you had his sister!"

"Don't worry," Alexi grunts. "He'll suffer plenty when he sees this one gutted like a fucking fish." He nudges me, and I struggle against his beefy body with absolutely zero luck.

Remy yells something in Russian. Xiomar and his men exchange confused looks. "What the hell are you saying?"

He grits his teeth. "Did you get him to wire the fucking money?"

Xiomar glares at Remy. "You give a lot of fucking orders, you know that? I don't see you doing anything right now. You show up late, leaving a goddamn mess behind you. Fucking asshole," he mutters under his breath, grabbing a laptop.

Remy lets go of me and stomps across the room, shoving

Xiomar away from the laptop. "Good for nothing guinea. I should have known you'd screw this up somehow. You beat him so hard, he can barely move. How the hell was this gonna work if you'd have killed him?" He stabs at some keys and drops it in Papa's lap. "Do it," he snarls right in his face. "Just hit the big red button and then we can move on."

Alexi presses the gun deeper into my back and my fingers twitch at my sides. "Payment," he hisses. "For the lives he stole. Lucky for us, you couldn't leave well enough alone. Always looking for the last word." He twists me around to face him. "You could say this is all your fault, Kat. If you'd have listened to your old man, this wouldn't be happening, and we'd have kept bleeding you dry a few drops at a time instead of blowing off all your heads at once." He grins. "But I like it better this way. We've been waiting a long time for this, and you helped us get it. *Sister*," he hisses.

"Don't you dare call me that!" A strangled cry escapes my lips, and I lash out, my fingernails dragging down the side of Alexi's face. My body is powered by pure adrenaline, and I don't stop for one second to think about what I'm doing. "You fucking monster!" I drive my knee into his balls with all of the force I can muster, sending him to the ground in a blubbering heap. His gun skitters across the floor and I lunge for it, closing my hand tight around the handle.

*Crack!*

One of Xiomar's men drops to the floor in front of me, and I point and pull the trigger, firing off two more quick shots. A loud crash registers amid all of the screaming in different languages as the laptop shatters on the floor. I point the gun to it and fire off another shot, watching the computer explode into thousands of tiny shards of glass and plastic.

"Kat! Get the hell out of here!" Rocco turns around and launches his arm backward, his fist cracking against Xiomar's jaw while Max leaps at Remy, pummeling him to the ground.

*Pop! Pop! Pop!*

More shots explode into the air, and Xiomar falls to the ground with a loud thud.

Loud voices come from the front of the bar, footsteps stomping through the place like herds of cattle when sirens blare in the distance. Whoever is left scatters like cockroaches, anxious to save their own asses.

I never thought I'd actually pray for cops to arrive at a scene where I have a gun in my hand, but I guess that's why they say never say never.

I drag myself over to Papa and fumble with the ties, my vision blurred with tears. "Papa," I whisper. "I'm going to get you out, okay? Please just stay with me. I'll get you out." I look around for something to cut them off and free him from the chair, but the tears fall too fast and I can't see anything in front of me except for blurs of color.

Red. Lots and lots of red.

"G-go," he rasps. "Don't save me. I-I don't want to be saved. I d-deserve this," he chokes, his voice garbled.

"No, Papa." My voice is low, thick with tears. I keep tugging and pulling, but my fingers can't work magic against the plastic zip ties.

Max has Remy backed against a wall, pounding the shit out of him with his fists, but Remy pushes him off and kicks Max clear across the room where he lands hard against the opposite wall, groaning and clutching his side. Remy grabs his gun off the floor and darts out of the room with Rocco on his heels.

The sirens get closer still, and I struggle to break my father free, sobs wracking my body. Strong hands cover mine and I look up to see Nico's face. "How the hell—?"

"Yeah, thanks for leaving me out there to rot," he says, taking the pocket knife from me and going to work on the ties.

"I don't understand. You weren't moving. Not breathing. I checked! It's not possible..."

He smirks at me. "Then consider me your guardian angel. Now get the fuck out there and stop that asshole who shot me from getting away." He nods over at Max. "Pull yourself together and get that shithead off the floor. We're gonna see how he likes being zip tied to a chair and then explaining to the cops why he's sitting here with mountains of heroin around him." Nico winks at Alexi who is groaning on the floor. "Looks like intent to sell in my opinion."

"Fuck you," Alexi grunts.

Nico presses a gun into my hand, and I run past Alexi, giving him a swift kick in the head for good measure. "I'd say I hope you get ass-rammed so hard in prison that you have dicks coming out of your mouth on the daily, but there's something else I'd rather say first." I lean in close. "Fuck you, asshole." I point the gun and fire at his balls. Once, twice, three times. The screams reverberate between the walls, and I smile. "That felt good. But this is gonna feel even better. For *me*." I fire off two more shots to the head...the one sitting on his shoulders.

Well, at least it used to sit there. Now it's kind of all over the place.

"Get my father out of here," I bark at Nico and Max. "I'm going for Remy."

I race around a corner, looking left and right. I see nothing. Hear nothing.

I edge around a wall, my arm pointed straight out in front of me. Time is short, and I need to find Rocco and bust the hell out of here before the cops show up. There is a shit ton of heroin here, and if we stay, we're screwed.

I kick open a door and swallow a gasp.

The dim light in the dingy room casts a shadow over Remy's face, making him look even more menacing, if that's possible. His lips curl into a sadistic smirk. "Tell me, Princess. Does he fuck you as good as I used to? Are you gonna be sad when I put a bullet in his brain? Because when he fucked with Cinque, he fucked with me, and that means he's a dead man." He cocks the gun in his hand, the one pressed against Rocco's head.

Rocco's breathing is labored because Remy's other hand is

tight around his neck. His fingers flex at his sides., his eyes wild, darting left and right. "Kat, get out of here," he rasps. "Get the guys and your dad out of here. It's okay."

My pulse throbs against my neck, fingertips numb and cold as they grip the gun tight. "This ends now, Remy."

"You're right about that, Princess. And let me tell you how it's gonna happen. I'm gonna shoot your boyfriend here in the head while you watch. And then when you fall apart, just like you did the first time, I'm gonna do what I should have done eight years ago and finish the job!"

He yanks Rocco's head to the side, and I meet his gaze. "Go," he mouths. "I love you."

"I love you, too," I whisper. "And I'm sorry. So, so sorry!"

*Bang! Pop! Crack!*

Remy flies backward, firing shots into the air as he crashes against the concrete. His head slams against the wall, blood oozing from the corners of his mouth as I pump bullets into his worthless, soulless body. Rocco crumbles to the floor next to him in a heap, a large, dark red stain seeping into the fabric of his shirt.

I pull the trigger over and over, emptying the clip into Remy, my first love and my worst nightmare. Every bullet that tears through his flesh erases more and more of the pain that I've carried around for all of these years until I'm finally empty.

Hollow.

Numb.

Blissfully so.

I've waited a long time to feel this way.

Revenge.

So bittersweet.

I thought it would heal me. I believed that it would fix what had long since been broken.

It didn't.

It doesn't give me the peace I'd always hoped for.

It doesn't make me any less sad.

It doesn't fill the gaping hole in my heart.

But it does make me realize what I have...and what I came so close to losing today.

It makes me feel less broken, more hopeful, and grateful for a life I have yet to live.

Bittersweet. It's the perfect description.

I step closer to Remy as he gasps and gurgles, flopping around like a fish out of water on the cold, hard floor. I make sure to fire a couple of bullets into his throat before I finish my assault, my shoulders heaving. I know his lungs are filling with blood, and that in minutes, he's going to drown in it.

It will be torture of the worst kind.

I kneel down next to him and whisper into his ear as he struggles to breathe. "'I've always wanted to look into the eyes of the person who murdered Mom and Lili and watch them die a horrible death that they suffered at my hand. I waited so long for this moment. I've planned it, obsessed about it, prayed for the opportunity. You think you took everything from me, but you didn't. Thank you for making me realize that I have more to live for. Thank you for giving me my life back." My voice cracks and I grab him by the chin to make sure he sees my lips form the next words. "Burn in hell, you motherfucker," I seethe as he spasms against the wall.

I leave him there, sputtering and gargling as death consumes him, and drop next to Rocco. I stroke the side of his pale face, gently tapping his cheek. His eyes flutter open after a minute or two. "You shot me," he mumbles.

I nod. "Yes. But I apologized to you before I did it."

"Was that supposed to make it more tolerable? Are you fucking crazy?"

"Some might say. But I knew that where I hit you wouldn't be fatal. I needed you out of the way so I could get to Remy. He was using you as a shield, and I needed him to let you go before I could take him out."

"What if I moved?"

I shrug. "You didn't."

"But I could have."

"Remy also could have shot me in the head once I pulled the trigger. He didn't."

"That was a pretty big risk."

"Luckily, it worked out in our favor, huh?"

"Guys! We need to get out of here! Did you off that sonofabitch yet or what, Kat?" Max comes running over, dropping to his knees next to us. "Jesus Christ, he shot Rocco?"

I shake my head. "No."

Max looks at me, a look of confusion shadowing his face. "Then who did?"

"She did," Rocco grunts, gritting his teeth as he shifts on the ground.

"Wow. That's some pretty fucked-up shit. Kat, you've got a lot of rage inside you, you know that?"

"I did what I needed to do." I lace my fingers with Rocco's. "Don't worry, you're going to be fine."

"I'm tired of playing target practice with you people. Why am I always the one getting shot?" Rocco grumbles.

"Because you're the one who always takes one for the team." I smile, tracing the outline of his lips with my finger.

"Great," he groans as Max loops an arm around him and slowly helps him to his feet. With a lot of effort, swearing, and panting, he finally straightens up enough to walk. Max and I hang on to either side of Rocco and lead him toward the back entrance through the room of death where, for a few minutes, I really thought we were going to lose this battle.

"Watch your step," Max grunts., shifting Rocco. "We've got a lot of brains and testicles decorating the floor in here, thanks to Kat. You do know one shot to the head would have done the trick, right?"

I snicker. "When do I ever do things the neat and clean way?"

"That's probably a better question for your guy here. He *is* your guy, yeah?" Max asks, a smile lifting his lips.

Rocco grunts and groans with each step. "Isn't it obvious I am? I mean, she fucking shot me today. First time we met, she put me in a chokehold. That's progress, don't you think? Natural progression and shit. At this rate, you'll be at my funeral next."

I look around at the bodies sprawled on the floor. Men who were supporting the fuckers who took Mom and Lili. Did they even know why they were here? Did they care? Or was it just about collecting the money?

"It's over, Kat," Rocco whispers, almost as if he can see the wheels turning in my mind. "It's finally over."

I nod. It is. Kind of. But there's one more loose end I need to tie up before I can really go on with my life. I have to hear it from Papa. Speaking of...

"Where's Papa?"

"Nico has him in a car up to Hoboken right now to see the Doc. That's where we're going. One of the guys from the Sardisco family was in the area and picked them up before the cops showed up."

"Why didn't he take his own car?" I furrow my brow.

"He gave his car to Sammy so he could get Lindy outta here. They grabbed her this morning. I'm gonna have a lot of shit to explain to her later."

I gasp. Lindy. "Oh my God, that poor thing. She must have been out of her mind. Jesus, this could have gone so bad, so fast."

"But it didn't," Rocco murmurs as Max hoists him up again, carrying him out of Red Square.

"Kat, where's his car?" Max huffs. "This guy is heavy, and I'm gonna collapse if I have to carry him much farther."

"Always so tough until you need to put the work in," Rocco jokes.

"I need a fucking hand truck," Max moans.

"I parked right around this corner." My throat tightens.

"With Alexi. Before Remy showed up and shot Nico right...there." I shake my head. "I still don't understand how—"

"Body armor." Max peeks his head over and winks at me. "He's the only one who wears it, though. You know, being the boss and all. I prefer to let my skills protect me," Max snickers as I unlock the doors with the key fob. He opens the back door and we slide Rocco into the backseat. I sit on one end of the seat with his head in my lap.

He looks at me, a pained look on his face. "It's gonna take me forever to get this blood cleaned up."

I smooth his hair back. "It's just a car. If I were you, I'd be happy that you're still alive to drive it."

Sirens blare from around the corner and squad cars zoom past us, surrounding Red Square. Max starts the car, waits for a beat, and then guns the engine. He stomps on the gas, blowing past the cars to get to the West Side Highway, and second by second, we get farther and farther away from my perpetual nightmare...the one it took me eight years to wake up from.

We escaped.

This time, and every time before it.

Trust, loyalty, *family*.

I've lamented the loss of it for so long, I never really took the time to notice it staring me in the face.

These guys would die for me. They'd do anything to protect me because they take care of their own, and I'm one of them. They've proven it again and again.

And I'd do the same for them.

Always.

It takes about twenty minutes to get to the Doc's place in Hoboken with the way Max drives. He pulls around the building and drives into the basement where we can use a private elevator without being seen by any nosy neighbors.

There are several drops of blood spotting the pavement, leading us to the elevator doors, and I know Papa is already here. I swallow hard. He's in great physical shape and can withstand a lot of trauma to the body, but they really went to work on him. God only knows what kind of damage they did.

Rocco hands me his phone when Max opens the back door. "Do me a favor and call my parents. Lindy is flipping the fuck out. She's texted me about fifty times in the past hour."

I lean down to graze his lips with mine. "Okay," I whisper. "I'll tell them you were a total hero who saved my life."

He winces as he sits up. "Totally worth it," he wheezes.

Max helps him stand up and walks him over to the elevator as I slide out behind them. I shut the door and pocket the keys before hoisting him over my arm. The elevator doors open and we slowly walk him inside. He grits his teeth. "Is someone gonna give me my own club for all the shit I put up with?"

"I don't know, man. You're being kind of a pussy right now, moaning and groaning like that. Strap on a pair and suck it up, huh?" Max winks at me over Rocco's head, and I roll my eyes.

*Ding!*

The elevator opens into the Doc's office. I've never been here before, but he's seen plenty of the Salesi family over the years and he even makes house calls from what I've heard. He's always on his game and completely trustworthy, two things that have made him a very rich, very irreplaceable, friend to the family.

"Nico had to leave for a little while to take care of something. He said to tell you he'd be back shortly," Doc says to us when he greets us by the elevator.

Doc is on the shorter side, kind of portly, with thick, dark hair and a dark mustache. He looks like one of the guys he treats, if I'm being honest. Warm smile, comforting voice, calm bedside manner. I love this guy already.

"And who is this beautiful woman?" He leans close to me. "You don't look Italian, dear."

"I'm not," I laugh. "Viktor is my father."

Doc nods. "I see. And these boys are treating you okay? Because if not," he shakes his head. "I know people."

I laugh. "They're good, don't worry. But thanks." My smile fades. "Is my father okay?"

Doc nods. "Yes, and I gave him something to help him rest. He's very lucky. He has a few broken ribs, lacerations to the face and body, and a shattered tibia. Nothing that won't heal in time. I'll be in after I take care of this guy." He looks at Rocco. "So, what number is this? Three, four? You keeping a collection of bullets? Making a charm bracelet out of them or something?"

Rocco groans, holding his side. "It's only two, Doc. I've been shot twice, okay? You know, not for nothing, everyone likes a little bit of ass, but nobody likes a smartass."

Doc chuckles and helps Rocco into one of the exam rooms, and I follow.

I help Doc ease Rocco onto the table and put a pillow under his head. Doc starts cleaning around his wound, and within a couple of minutes, Rocco has an IV in his arm and a sedative flowing into his veins. He looks up at me, a goofy smile on his face.

"Oh, you're feeling no pain now, huh?" I run a hand through his hair and look at Doc.

He grins. "You have about five minutes."

I nod. "Okay."

He steps out and closes the door behind him.

I lace my fingers with Rocco's and let out a deep sigh. "I can't believe it's finally over."

"What is?" Rocco's eyes are heavy. "Did Doc fix me up yet? Can we go home?"

I giggle. Doc must have pumped him up good. "No, he hasn't even started."

"Oh." Rocco's eyes droop a little. "This shit is awesome. I can't feel my legs right now."

"You rest now, okay?" I smooth his hair back and kiss the tip of his nose. "I'll work you out plenty when you're back to normal."

"Mnphoboohh." He breathes.

"I love you, too," I whisper.

I walk into the waiting room. "I think he's ready, Doc."

He snickers. "Yep. Right on time." Doc pats me on the shoulder and closes the door behind him, leaving me alone with Max.

He puts his hand on my shoulder. "You okay? It's over, Kat. Really and truly."

I let out a deep breath and rub the back of my neck. It's stiff as hell from all of the stress. "I know. I just...there's a lot that I still need to take care of, though."

Max nods his head. "I'll be honest, I don't know much, but I do know you lost your mom and sister, and I'm really sorry about that. It's a horrible thing to lose people so close to you like that."

I nod. "It's this life, you know? There are lots of benefits, but they come with a lot of risk and danger." I shudder thinking about how I might have lost Papa and Rocco today, too. "It's not worth it, you know?"

Max nods. "Yeah. I've had the same thought about a million times. But we don't get to choose. We just inherit shit."

"Yeah..." I manage a half-smile for him. "And Sloane, she's okay with that?"

He shrugs. "Nah, but she can't get enough of the spicy Italian sausage. I can't blame her."

I giggle and give him a punch in the shoulder. "You guys and your sausages."

"You know you like it. Don't play like you don't know what I'm talking about."

Heat rises into my cheeks, and I curl my toes in my flip-flops. Damn, they're really freaking cold. I could use some of that heat in my feet right about now.

It's a first for me. I don't usually make kills in workout wear and flip-flops. It's a lot more comfortable, if I'm being honest. Sneakers would have made it even better.

"I know he really cares about you. He's a good guy. Not the top enforcer, though. I don't give a fuck what Nico says."

"Don't be jealous. It's not a good color for you."

Max flashes a crooked grin. "Hey, listen, I'll make the call to his family. You go see your Pops, okay?"

I nod and hand him the phone. "Thank you," I whisper. "For everything."

He winks at me and waves the phone. "No need to thank me. It's what we do for family, Kat."

I have to bite my lip to keep it from quivering as I open the door to Papa's room. Jesus, I used to be so cold, so tough. What the hell happened to me? Is this really what love does to you? Makes you all fucking soft and...blech...*emotional*?

The door creaks open and Papa's eyes flutter open. "Katarina," he mumbles, his voice thick with fatigue. "Are you okay?"

"Yes, Papa. I'm fine." I lean over the side of the bed and put my hands over his bandaged ones. "How are you feeling?"

"Eh. I've had better days." He turns his head slightly to look at me, his eyes crinkling in the corners. "But we won."

"This time," I murmur, dropping my eyes to the white bed sheet.

"Katarina, I'm so sorry for not being honest with you about what happened. I was afraid it would drive you away when I needed to keep you close. Safe. Protected."

"I carried so much guilt for the past eight years, Papa. I blamed myself. I thought you blamed me, too, and that's why you wouldn't talk to me. I knew I was a constant reminder of them being gone, especially Lili. I just wish—" I grit my teeth as a single tear slips from the corner of my eye.

Goddammit. Here we go again.

"I should have been honest with you, but you were so angry. I was afraid of what you'd do if you knew the truth about what really happened, and that I'd lose you, too. It was wrong. All of it. And I regret my decisions every day that goes by. I took what didn't belong to me, and I paid the price. We all did." He raises a hand to my face. "I hate myself for that," he croaks. "I was hungry and could never get my fill of anything that fed my power. The consequences..." He pauses, his blue eyes pooling with tears. "Were dire. But I gambled anyway. And lost almost everything in the process."

"I just can't believe I didn't see it. Alexi... He was like a brother to me. You took him in, cared for him like he was your own, and he was going to kill us!"

"I destroyed his life. I deserved to be punished. I kept him away from his family, I threatened that if they tried to contact him, I'd kill him." Papa lets out a deep sigh. "And all of it was to protect you. Alexi was the leverage I needed to keep you alive, but after Raines..." He sighs. "I told you there would be hell to pay after that."

"Yeah, well, you were right about *that*." I pick at the edge of the sheet. "I need you to agree to something. Right here. Right now."

"Anything."

"You promise that you'll always be honest with me, no matter what. You need to promise that you won't just leave me again, that you'll always be here for me. Because..." My throat tightens, and I swallow hard past the growing lump that's managed to lodge itself there. "Because I can't lose you, too, okay? I almost did. I almost lost so much today."

"I know. And I do promise you...all of it. Everything."

"And starting next year, we need a new birthday tradition, okay? No more of you running away, got it? We will deal with things together, like a real family."

Papa nods. "That sounds like a good plan." He strokes the side of my face. "I love you, and I can see that Rocco was the right man for the job after all."

I furrow my brow. "Right man for what job?"

"For handling *you*." Papa manages a small smile which I can make out through all of the gauze wrapped around his face and head. "Nico assured me he was the guy, that he'd take care of you no matter what."

I nod. "I shot him today."

"And here you are telling me about it. Mission accomplished." Papa strokes the side of my face and I place a hand over it.

"I love him, Papa."

"I can tell." He smiles. "I hope he knows what he's getting himself into with you."

"I think he's got a good idea considering he's now in surgery to remove that bullet of mine." I lean over to kiss my father's forehead. "I love you, too, Papa."

"I know. And I love you. I should have told you that every day for the past eight years to make sure you heard it and believed it. You're everything to me, and all I have left."

"Yeah, and don't you forget it," I whisper with a quick sniffle. I know what's coming next, and I don't like it at all.

More tears. *Again?* I just can't. It's getting a little ridiculous now.

One day I'm a lethal assassin, and the next, an emotional train wreck.

This is my evolution?

*Really?*

# EPILOGUE

## One Year Later

I twirl around, pale pink tulle fluttering softly around me. The bodice is snug all the way to my waist and the tops of my boobs peek out of the deep neckline. I lift an eyebrow at my reflection and do another half-twist in front of the mirror.

"You look gorgeous!" Shaye squeals, gathering up the beaded white skirt of her wedding dress and dancing around me. "That color is just perfect for you!"

I wrinkle my nose and fluff out the full skirt. "Pink, huh? I kinda hoped for black leather instead when you asked me to be a bridesmaid."

Sloane giggles, holding her hair on top of her head. "How very BDSM of you. Are you thinking we'd carry whips and chains instead of flowers?"

I smirk. "The guys sure would love that."

Shaye holds out her champagne flute and the salesgirl pours her another glass. "Oh my God, I love the dress even more now that it's on you!"

I roll my eyes at Sloane. "We really need to go dress shopping when she's good and sober, you know?"

The bell hanging over the boutique door jingles and I bite my lower lip when I see Rocco walk over toward us, his hands stuck in his pockets and that sexy grin on his face. "So, you've got my girl all wrapped up in pink lace, huh?" He winks at me. "Are you twitching underneath it all? How's it feel to wear an actual color, babe? An outfit that's not all black?"

"I voted against it, but it looks like I'm outnumbered." I shrug. "I guess I can be girly for one day."

He inches closer until the fresh scent of his cologne wafts under my nose. His fingertips dance down the side of my arm, making my skin pebble with goosebumps. "You're beautiful," he murmurs.

"Thanks." I stroke the back of his neck and pull him toward me, plastering my lips against his. Mmm. So soft, so sweet, so perfect.

I could stand here all day and never tire of his mouth, hot and hungry against mine.

Shaye clears her throat behind us. "Um, do you guys want to take this into the fitting room or something?"

It kills me to break this kiss, but she's right. It would be much more appropriate to lock ourselves into one of the fitting rooms.

"Is that allowed?" he whispers, his forehead pressed against mine.

I smirk at him. "Didn't you get your fill this morning?"

"Never." He presses his lips to my forehead and smacks me on the ass when I gather my skirt and turn toward the fitting room to get the hell out of this ball of pink fluff. "I feel like the stick cotton candy is wound around." I grunt, tripping over the bottom of the dress.

"Ohhh, you had to go there, didn't you?" Rocco groans. "Now I need to go out and buy some cotton candy for later. Let's see if we can recreate that feeling, huh?"

Shaye snorts into her flute before sucking it all down in one large gulp. "My, my, my. Feeling frisky, are we? Maybe you need to take her to Culaccino," she says to Rocco with a knowing grin.

I roll my eyes and close the fitting room door, sliding this monstrosity over my head and pulling on my leather leggings and black v-neck. I let out a sigh of relief once the transformation is complete.

So much better.

I pull open the door to find the three of them huddled together, whispering conspiratorially. I creep toward them and whisper, "What are we talking about?"

They jump apart, guilty looks on their faces. "Oh, um, well we were just talking about how I think we should wear flats for the wedding. You know, it'll be more comfortable." Shaye grins at me. "We'll be dancing and on our feet all day, so really, it makes sense."

My mouth drops open. "First, the dress and now...*flats?*" I barely choke out the word and they all erupt into laughter.

"Kat, you're a cowgirl now. Are you ever going to ditch the stilettos?"

"You know Jimmy Choo makes cowgirl boots, don't you?" Rocco asks with a smirk. "And she's got 'em in every color."

Sloane shakes her head. "Well, I was a fan of the flats," she says. "Just so you know, that's how we're rolling in when Max and I get hitched. Prepare yourself, girl."

"I don't care if I'm two feet taller than all of you. I'm wearing heels. Period. No negotiation."

Rocco snickers. "You know what she'll do if you piss her off. I think we've all seen her wrath in action."

"I'll take it into consideration." Shaye winks at us.

He snakes an arm around my waist. "I hate to break up the party, but I need this gorgeous woman for a meeting."

"Sure, *meeting*." Sloane laughs. "We know what that's code for!"

I snuggle close to Rocco as he leads me out the boutique entrance. "Nice work. Very smooth."

"I got your S.O.S. text. I can be a wingman when I need to be." He pulls open the door to his Maserati, and Stoli 2 leaps at me from the backseat. His tail is wagging so hard and fast, he almost takes me out with it. I giggle and give him a good rub under his chin, just the way he likes.

"I think he misses the farm." I smile. "Don't you, boy? We'll be back up there in a few days, okay?"

Rocco starts the car and merges onto the road. "I wasn't actually full of shit back there. Nico wants to discuss a few things about the operations up there. And he's working with a few breeders. We might be getting more horses sooner rather than later."

"We might have to expand faster than we thought." I hug Stoli 2 around the neck. "But Papa is happy. Everyone is making shit loads of money, and we have our own little love nest in the boonies where nobody bothers us and we're hidden away from the crazy that used to be our life." I reach down and give his leg a little squeeze. "It's perfect. For me, anyway." I look over at him. "But what about you? Do you miss the action down here? Do you feel like you're disconnected, being so far away?"

"Hold that thought for a minute, would you?"

I nod as he pulls into the back parking lot of my favorite pizzeria, Villa Laura. "What are we doing here? I thought you said we were meeting with Nico's dad?"

"Yup."

"Oh, lunch meeting. Okay. Is that why you parked in the back?" I snicker. "So nobody sees the car and guesses what we're doing here with him?"

"Something like that." Rocco gets out and Stoli 2 jumps out after him. He jogs around the front of the car, opens my door, and holds out his hand. I grasp it and he pulls me up, gently grazing my lips with his. "You hungry?" he asks.

"Starving. Although that birthday breakfast was certainly filling," I reply with a waggle of my eyebrows.

"Wait until you see what I have planned for dinner."

"Mmm, I *can't* wait."

He squeezes my hand. "Just a little while longer, and we'll be outta here."

"Promise?"

"Would I ever lie to you?"

I cock an eyebrow, and he laughs. "I meant, *again?*" He pulls open the back entrance to the pizzeria. I step into the darkness behind him. "Why is it so dark?" I whisper, my foot slipping on something splashed across the floor. "Ugh, it must be pizza grease," I groan. "All over my new—"

Rocco flips a switch on the wall next to me, illuminating a single, candle-lit table in the middle of a room. A large pizza sits on a pedestal in the center of it, surrounded by black and white calla lilies, and a bottle of Stoli vodka.

I gasp, a hand flying up to my mouth. "Oh my God, what is this?"

Rocco shrugs. "I figured we'd have our own private meeting first. With pizza. And shit vodka."

I run up to the table. *Happy Birthday, Kat* is spelled out in pepperoni and black olives. I spin around to leap into Rocco's arms, but he's no longer behind me. No, now he's kneeling on the floor next to me. Next to Stoli 2. Both stare up at me with an expectant look in their eyes.

As Rocco holds out a big ass diamond ring.

My heart thuds against my chest so hard, I'm sure he can see it protruding from my chest. "Holy shit," I whisper, falling to my knees next to him.

He grins. "You're not supposed to be down here."

Tears pool in the corner of my eyes. "I want to be wherever you are."

"That's a really good thing," he murmurs. "Because I want the exact same thing." He holds up the ring in front of me. "You see this? I'm giving this to you today for a couple of different reasons. First, because I'm fucking crazy about you and I need you in my life. Forever."

I nod my head, blinking fast to keep the tears in place.

"Second, I wanted to bring you back to the place where you

pretty much stole my heart. This is where we first met, do you remember? You nearly killed me?"

I sniffle, swiping at the rogue tears that managed to escape. "You were such a baby about it."

"Yeah, cutting off my airway does things to a man, what can I say? He chuckles. "And third, I decided you needed some new memories of this day. Happy ones with lots of pictures you'll smile and laugh at for years to come. It's a new year for you and for us. We're only looking forward, you and me, you got that?"

"Yes," I whisper, a sob catching in my throat.

"So, Katarina Ivanov, would you make me the happiest man on Earth and say yes to forever with me?"

I throw my arms around him, blubbering like a little bitch.

Again.

It's my new look, I guess.

I'd better get used to it.

"I will. And I do." I hug him tight around the neck. "I love you so much, babe."

"I love you, too." He rises to his feet and pulls me up to meet his knowing gaze. "But there's more..." He nods at the door to our left. "In five...four...three...two...one..."

"Surprise!"

The door swings open and swarms of people pile into the room, swooping around us. We're assaulted by bear hugs, kisses, and yelps of excitement, and I couldn't be happier. Stoli 2 jumps on all of our guests, licking them like they're hiding bacon up their sleeves. Shaye, Sloane, and Allegra run right over to me, squealing and shrieking their congratulations and best wishes, while Antonio, Max, and Nico slap Rocco on the back, joking about the last man standing.

But something...someone...is missing from the action.

Lindy.

My throat tightens. Hearing that she'd been lied to for pretty much her entire life after being kidnapped and held at gunpoint was too much for Lindy to handle and she just up and left. She's out in California now, far away from all of the people who'd deceived her. It didn't matter that they were only trying to protect her. It was a life she wanted no part of ever again. The family has been trying hard to rekindle a relationship with her and they miss her terribly, but she's still shut down.

I understand her need for space, but I really hope that she comes around and realizes what she left behind.

For everyone's sakes.

I walk over to the corner where Papa is standing. "I'm so glad you're here, Papa. It really means a lot to me."

He strokes the side of my face. "I'll never leave you again, Katarina. That, I promise you."

"Vik, glad you made it." Rocco shakes Papa's hand. "I guess that means you like me now, huh?"

Papa rolls his eyes. "Are you going to ask me that every time I see you?"

"Until you give me the answer I wanna hear, yeah. I will." He turns to me and winks. "I'll get him to say it before the wedding. I'm persistent like that."

I give Papa a stern look, and his grin deepens. "What?" he asks. "I like keeping him on his toes."

"Ah, see, we're making progress! He used the word 'like' in a sentence about me!" He winks at Papa. "Don't worry, Papa. I grow on everyone."

Papa lifts an eyebrow. "Yes, like a fungus." Then his stoic look is replaced by a wide smile. Papa grins at Rocco and holds out his hand. "Congratulations. I know you'll take good care of my daughter."

Rocco just stares at it. Then he looks up and shakes his head. "Nah. This is how we do it in my family." And he throws his arms around my father, tightening them until Papa reluctantly does the same. He's never really been the type to engage in public displays of affection.

Or any displays, for that matter.

But my fiancé doesn't care. I've never seen him so lit up, and it feels amazing.

Because he's this lit up over *me*.

"Yeah!" Rocco exclaims, slapping him on the back. "I got a hug! Progress!"

"My two favorite men." I let out an exaggerated sigh. "This sure is going to be a fun ride."

Rocco grabs me around the waist and spins me around as Viktor joins the rest of the party.

"Fun *ride*...fucking A, yeah! Let's table that one for later." He winks at me and smacks my ass for the second time that day. He loves the sound his hand makes against the leather. "And don't forget about the cotton candy."

**If you loved the MOB LUST series, you won't want to miss the spin-off SEVERINOV BRATVA series featuring Kat's sexy and sadistic Russian cousins!**

**MERCILESS is up next! You can check out the blurb below!**
**Click here to read it now on Amazon!**

---

***I'm A Ruthless Killer, A Bloodthirsty Beast.***
I always take what I want, what I'm owed, and what has been stolen from me.
With a gorgeous face and a porn-star body, Lindy thinks she owns Sin City. But my new obsession made a deadly choice when she walked into my casino.
She trusted the wrong people, put greed before common sense, and lost everything.
Now, there's a debt to be paid.
To me.
But I don't care about money.

I want her as my payment.
And it's time to collect.

———

**And if you love sexy and seductive enemies to lovers and friends to lovers romance, don't miss Kristen's LOVE DRUNK series! Check out Chris and Mia in YOU BELONG WITH ME next!
Read it now on Amazon!**

———

**Stay up-to-date on new releases by joining Kristen's reader group on Facebook or signing up for her newsletter.**
**Facebook Reader Group:** http://bit.ly/2iQBr5V
**Newsletter Sign-Up:** https://bit.ly/2Jubp8h

## MOB LUST SERIES

### Dark Italian Mafia Romance

*SCREWING THE MOB*

***RULING THE MOB***

## *BETRAYING THE MOB*

## *SLAYING THE MOB*

***CRUSHING THE MOB***

## SEVERINOV BRATVA SERIES

### Dark Russian Mafia Romance

*MERCILESS*

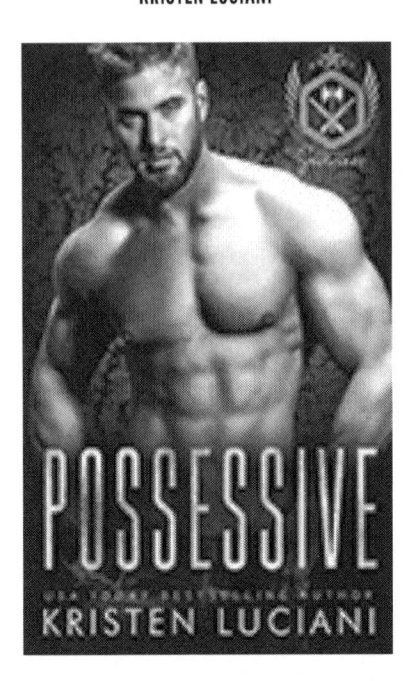

***POSSESSIVE***

## *VENGEFUL*

## *RAVAGE*

## MEN OF MAYHEM SERIES

### Dark Italian Mafia Romance

**MAYHEM**

**WANTED**

## *COVETED*

## *TAKEN*

## LOVE DRUNK SERIES

*YOU BELONG WITH ME*
*BOOK ONE OF THE LOVE DRUNK SERIES*

***NOT OVER YOU***
***BOOK TWO OF THE LOVE DRUNK SERIES***

***JUST SAY YES***
***BOOK THREE OF THE LOVE DRUNK SERIES***

***BEFORE YOU GO***
***BOOK FOUR OF THE LOVE DRUNK SERIES***

## STANDALONE ROMANCE TITLES

**DIRTY, DARK, & DANGEROUS**

***PLOWED***

## *FATAL LIES*

## *DIRTY REVENGE*

*JUST LUST*

## *LIGHT ME UP*

### **WRAPPED IN LOVE**

***DONUT TEASE ME***

## ABOUT THE AUTHOR

Kristen Luciani is a *USA Today* bestselling romance author and momtrepreneur with a penchant for stilettos, Silicon Valley, plunging necklines and grapefruit martinis. As a deep-rooted romantic who prefers juicy drama to fill the lives of anyone other than her, she tried her hand at creating a world of enchantment, sensuality, and intrigue, finally uncovering her true passion. No pun intended...

**Connect With Kristen**
**Facebook:** http://on.fb.me/1Y87KjV
**Instagram:** https://instagram.com/kristen_luciani
**BookBub:** https://bit.ly/2FIcoP1
**Facebook Reader Group:** http://bit.ly/2iQBr5V
**Newsletter:** https://bit.ly/2Jubp8h

---

**Want a FREE book? Check out Kristen's sexy romantic suspense story, OUT OF ORDER!**
<u>Click here to download!</u>

Made in United States
Orlando, FL
03 June 2022